WOLVES OF WINTER

R. Allen Chappell

Dedication

This book is dedicated to those Diné who still follow the Beauty Way, and while their numbers are less each year, they remain the well from which the people draw strength and feed the *Hozo* that binds them together.

Acknowledgments

Again, many sincere thanks to those Navajo friends and classmates who provided "grist for the mill." Their insight into Navajo thought and reservation life helped fuel a lifelong interest in their culture, one I once only observed from the other side of the fence.

Author's Note

In the back pages you will find a small glossary of Navajo words and terms used in this story, the spelling of which may vary somewhat, depending on which expert's opinion is referenced.

Table of Contents

1075 A.D.

Winter settled in late, and with a vengeance; blizzard after blizzard howled through the canyons, leaving deep snow to hinder travel and make difficult the collection of firewood or hunting. By the month of popping trees even the oldest could not remember it ever being so cold.

And it was then the wolves of winter appeared, first only one or two watching silently from the other side of the canyon, finally shrugging deep into their blankets they went away. This village on the cliff was not like those to the north—this one might not be so easy.

1

The Runner

When Harley Ponyboy looked up from his digging it was through a haze, forcing him to crane his neck for a breath of fresh air. The dust of a thousand years hung over the *kiva*—the dust of dead people—and there was no escaping it. A fine powder already coated the neckerchief over his nose though only mid-morning and the real work yet to come. "I wish't we had enough water ta sprinkle down this dirt." He coughed, nearly choking on his own words.

His friend Thomas Begay straightened, and adjusted his own bandanna, leaving just his eyes visible below the brim of his hat. He licked his parched lips and scanned the far rim. "Maybe it'll rain…it's for damn sure time." He saw little sign of it even to the southwest. Down in Mexico the Baja was stingy with its clouds, squeezing them dry against the rocky peaks, leaving only shadows to sail north.

Under the neckerchief Harley ran the tip of his tongue across his teeth. "Rain? Maybe…" he said, "maybe." He was not one to waste words on anything so unlikely. His back hurt, stiff and sore from the previous day's dig—sweat mixed with dirt caked mud at the corners of his eyes. He was rethinking this job of excavating a ruin. It was not only the heat and the dust, but the sobering thought that a dead person might pop up at any moment. True, they had been dead a very long time, and their *chindi,* if they had one, were probably weak and tired. Still, the old people believed these ancients were best left alone. "They still have their powers," they said, "That's why witches collect their old bones and grind them into evil potions."

Thomas Begay pursed his lips and narrowed his eyes against the shimmering heat. *What the hell is that?* he wondered, focusing on a scraggly line of trees across the canyon. He nudged his friend, "Harley, take a look at that little crap-bunch of cedars right across from us. Is there something moving along there…or is the sun getting to me?"

Harley, known to have extraordinary vision when sober, screwed up his face, squinted and blinked a few times to clear the dust. "It's a man," he whispered… "Running…he's *running*." Harley kept his eyes on the spot even as the runner momentarily disappeared into a draw. Lifting a plastic jug of water he took a long swallow, passed it to Thomas, and observed, "Indian…or he better be if he's goin' ta get very far in this heat."

Thomas Begay studied a long moment before murmuring, almost to himself, "Why would anyone be running in this heat?"

Harley grinned behind his kerchief. "Maybe there's a bear down there in the brush. I'm told they come here for the chokecherries this time a year. Maybe he was picking chokecherries and ran across a bear."

The two Navajo watched and pondered the possibilities. *What might cause a man to be running in the heat of the day, and so far from anywhere, too?* Before either of them could conjure up a tolerable explanation the faint wail of a siren drifted down-canyon. Neither man bothered to turn or look in that direction, but Thomas Begay grinned as the answer finally came to him. He canted his head slightly and gestured with a thumb over his shoulder. "That might explain it." Neither he, nor Harley was a stranger to sirens, and Indians running from the law were not uncommon. The two men looked again in the direction of the runner and wondered if it was someone they might know; both men were well acquainted in the area and several likely suspects leapt to mind. The distant figure, now only a speck, soon faded into the wavering vista, and the two *Diné* reluctantly turned back to their shovels.

After a few minutes Harley lifted his hat, and wiping his forehead on his sleeve, gazed through the junipers below the alcove at the professor's horse-trailer. His mule Jake, an ungainly creature by any measure, stood tied and asleep on his feet...one ear twitched occasionally to ward off an imaginary fly. Harley had given very little for the animal despite knowing one generally gets what he pays for when it comes to mules. They are a tribe known to harbor more than a few chancy characters. Harley, however, was convinced there was more to this mule than met the eye. Professor Custer hemmed and hawed but in the end agreed he could bring the animal along, thinking it would give his old friend something to do in his spare time...something that didn't involve drinking. And too, the mule did have its uses, packing equipment up to the dig...and only the day before helped pull a large sandstone slab away from the entrance to the village.

Dr. Custer and Harley at one time were drinking companions. That was before the professor decided to take charge of his life. The archaeologist still considered Harley more friend than employee and was prone to humor the little man in that way. Harley did occasionally fall off the wagon, but it had been some time. George Custer could only hope for the best.

A gradual increase in the siren's volume now warned the diggers to expect a visitor. Again the pair welcomed the distraction. The two men leaned on their shovels and their previous conjecture regarding the identity of the fugitive turned now to the identity of the pursuer, who they were also likely to know, both men having a good bit of experience with the local law.

Having found police sirens to be a disruptive force among his Navajo workmen, Professor George Armstrong Custer hurried from his tent and did not look happy as he came. His "Contract Archaeology" venture had been lucky to snare this project but was barely able to stay ahead of the road crew. A new startup company had lately beaten his bids leaving the professor at a loss to know how the newcomers could possibly make any money with such proposals. Even with just Thomas and Harley working he would be lucky to come out ahead on this project.

Thomas adjusted his bandanna, nudged Harley, and smiled across the dig as the professor precariously navigated the rubble, several times nearly losing his balance. The long-legged *Diné* shook his head, climbed out of the excavation, then turned and offered his shorter companion a hand up. Harley scrambled out of the hole releasing an even denser cloud of dust. The two fell in with the professor and all three picked their way down to the site of the proposed highway. The old road was to be rerouted through the canyon, paved and a passing lane added should funds hold out. A greater general awareness of the damage caused by these road projects had, of late, been a concern among those government officials charged with protecting such sites. Even lesser oil-field roads took their toll and many a dozer operator took home a little prize or two from time to time. The upshot was contracts with accredited archaeologists to survey and recover whatever was thought to be of scientific or cultural importance.

When Officer Billy Red Clay slid his tribal unit to a stop in a spray of gravel it was clear the generally unflappable young policeman was in a temper. George Custer and his two workmen watched through the SUV's window as Billy spoke a few harsh words into a microphone before throwing open the door. A nasty cut above his right eye was already beginning to swell and turn blue at the edges. Blood dribbled down the side of his face leaving a dark stain on the collar of his uniform. When the tribal policeman recognized his Uncle Thomas Begay and his friend Harley Ponyboy, even with the bandanas over their noses, he straightened his hat and feigned non-chalance. "You boys out robbing banks this morning?"

Thomas Begay smiled at his Nephew's attempt to make light of an obviously embarrassing situation. "No, but we might take up that line of work if it gets any hotter out here today." He didn't smile when he asked, "Who are you looking for Nephew?"

The policeman hesitated only a moment. "That Hopi boy, Danny Hat... The Feds have a warrant out for him and left a message for someone at Tribal to pick him up." Billy Red Clay didn't look well...not well at all. He sighed, "I guess the dispatcher thought that meant me."

"Danny Hat?" Harley pushed forward. "What's he done now? He's goin' ta kill his mother if he don't straighten out. I been knowin' him since he was little and it's just one thing after the other with that boy."

Billy Red Clay shook his head causing a stabbing pain to make his swollen eye twitch. "Dispatch didn't say what it was about, Harley, but its FBI...something serious I expect. Those boys mostly just handle homicides here on the reservation." The officer paused and for a moment looked doubtful. "I suppose he could be a witness or something, though."

Thomas Begay broke into a grin and pushed his chin toward his nephew's bad eye. "I wouldn't think Danny Hat would be *that* hard to catch."

Billy attempted a smile. "He wasn't that hard to catch Uncle...at least not the first time. I had him cuffed and in the patrol car, meek as a lamb. He didn't offer no resistance. But that was up at the road construction where he works. I don't know...maybe he didn't want to show his ass in front of the crew."

Billy swayed back on his heels leaning against his car for support. "As soon as we dropped down over the hill he said he had to take a leak…and could I let him out to do it. Said he had to go real bad and if I didn't let him out he would just piss in his pants. Headquarters just issued me this unit—it's the first one I ever had that didn't smell like piss—so I let him out and re-cuffed his hands in front so he could go." Billy's voice grew uncertain. "The little bastard was standing behind the door doing his business when all of a sudden he slams the door into me. Knocked me flat on my back!" Billy fingered the growing lump above his eye and winced at the touch. "I guess I was knocked a little silly for a minute 'cause when I gathered myself he was hightailing it down over the edge. I knew I was too woozy to catch him on foot and figured I would try to get ahead of him." Billy stopped to catch his breath and fixed Harley with his one good eye. "You haven't seen him, have you?"

Harley gave a slight push of his lips toward the far side of the canyon.

"How long ago?" Billy seemed wobbly and even more dependent on the car.

Harley looked down. "We don' know if it was even him, Billy."

Thomas Begay spoke up, "No more'n ten minutes I'd guess, but he's already across the draw and up the other side. You'll play hell catching him afoot in your shape." Thomas knew Harley hated to put the finger on anyone, but it didn't bother him any. Thomas had never really cared for Danny Hat, and he wasn't going to lie to a clan member, and his own nephew at that—not to protect someone he cared

7

nothing about. That he really didn't know it was Danny Hat didn't deter him in the least. *How many runners could be on the loose in this heat?*

Harley glanced at Professor Custer then at the ground as he pulled off his bandanna and sighed softly, "I'll go get him Billy—if the Doc will let me—I got my mule over there and I have known the boy a long time…I expect I can get him all right." He stopped and thought for a moment. "He didn' take your pistol did he Billy?"

The officer attempted a smile. "Harley if he had taken my pistol he'd probably already shot me." He shook his head and turned so Harley could see his holstered sidearm, then passed a hand across his face and again winced as he brushed the cut. "There was something not right about that boy." He spit into the sand. "I don't know…maybe he was just scared."

The professor, who had been standing back listening, frowned and spoke in a low voice, "Harley if you think you can bring him back without anyone getting hurt go ahead. I suppose that would be better than calling in more people and making a circus out of it. I don't want to lose any more time on this job than we have to. We're barely keeping ahead of the highway department as it is."

Just as the professor said this a white Chevy one-ton in bad need of a wash, came rattling off the grade in low gear. There were two rough looking men inside and when they stepped down from the truck the smaller one called out, "How you boys doin' today?" As they drew nearer he could see the policeman's swollen eye and grinned. "Not so good I guess."

The second man peered into the empty patrol car. "What did you do with Danny Hat?" He was a large man, white, and apparently used to talking down to Indians.

Thomas Begay bristled then moved closer, wondering if the heat had caused the man to abandon his manners. He wasn't one to be intimidated by rough talk and knew Billy Red Clay wasn't either. The two of them stared at the big man. It was only then Thomas recognized him as the construction supervisor and foreman for the road crew—probably Danny Hat's boss. His name was Karl Hoffman and he had been pushing the professor to hurry the recovery effort since the project began. The two of them had words early on, and had not seen eye to eye since.

George Custer folded his arms across his chest and eyed Hoffman with a glint in his eye. "Karl, Officer Red Clay is in charge here, and I think you'd better keep that in mind."

The big man, still thinking he had the advantage, took a more aggressive posture. "Look here Custer, I'm already short an operator as it is, and now this." He wasn't pleased to lose an operator, especially one carried off without explanation. "Now I'm the only operator left to run that dozer."

The supervisor had been working the bulldozer when his employee was taken away, and missed the arrest entirely. He felt he might have, somehow, interceded on his man's behalf. Not being allowed that chance angered him and his voice took an edge, "That boy was bundled off before I even knew what the problem was." Hoffman was determined to know why, and grew more belligerent as he turned back to

Billy Red Clay. Raising his voice, he balled his fists and moved forward a step, growling, "Where's my man? I won't ask you again. You took him! Where is he?" At this, his companion began to edge forward, and Thomas Begay, who was known to have a short fuse, moved to intercept him. The professor caught his arm and shook his head. George Custer didn't want to lose any of his own workers if he could help it—he also knew that might be the least of it should Thomas get out of hand.

Billy Red Clay's head hurt and this man's tough talk was trying his patience. He took a half step toward the foreman with an open hand held in front of him; the other hand hovered over the butt of his service revolver. "You! Stand down! Or by God I'll take the both of you in along with Danny Hat...when I catch him again." The lawman cocked his head to one side and glared with his one good eye. "I'll not have you disrespect this badge, or me. You're on the reservation...and I'm the law here today."

The big foreman faltered and hesitated as he noticed Harley Ponyboy coming around the corner of the horse trailer with a tire iron in his hand. None of these Navajos seemed intimidated and there were more of them than he first thought, too. He dropped his gaze to the badge on Billy Red Clay's shirt and murmured, "I guess you don't have Danny anyway..." Hoffman motioned to his companion and the pair backed up a step before turning toward their truck. The foreman called back over his shoulder. "We'll see what the Colorado State Patrol has to say about this...I'm not so sure were still on the Navajo reservation. This could be Ute land."

"I'm the Law here right now," Billy said calmly and without raising his voice, "You call who you please."

Thomas smiled. His nephew had conducted himself well to his way of thinking and he now thought a little more of Billy Red Clay's chosen profession. He had once felt the boy too good-natured to make a lawman, now he could see that might not be the case after all.

Harley, who had been watching the entire exchange from across his saddle, smiled to himself, and was glad it worked out as it did. He knew from experience Thomas had the ability to turn an iffy situation into a full-blown disaster in the blink of an eye.

Billy Red Clay, with a final glance at the retreating road workers, turned to the others and scratched his chin. "For just a minute there I thought I might have to pull a gun on the man...I've never had to pull a gun on anyone before."

Thomas chuckled, "Well, I'm glad you didn't nephew, none of our clan has shot a white man in over a hundred years..." He stopped and thought a moment. "Well...except for Hector Bitsillie who shot a couple of Italian deserters in World War ll. He later said that was mostly an accident—it was dark, and he thought at the time they might be Germans."

Billy Red Clay shrugged, and with a lopsided grin looked past the mule at Harley Ponyboy. "You better get moving Harley, that Hopi isn't going to catch himself."

Harley smirked and snorted as he and Thomas readied the mule.

George Custer brought Billy Red Clay a drink of water and whispered, "Well done young man."

Thomas finished the saddling and opened the trailer's tack compartment for another plastic jug of water, looping the saddle strings through the handle. "I figure one of you boys might need a drink before this is over." He knew Harley wasn't one to quit an enterprise once started and it was doubtful he would find much water in the direction he was headed. Danny Hat was young and tough and regardless of how well Harley thought he knew him, it might take more than just *talking* to bring him back. When Thomas thought about it, Harley was never that good a talker anyway. But he had no worries about the little man handling the fugitive should it come to a fight. Despite his size Harley Ponyboy had surprised more formidable opponents than Danny Hat.

Billy Red Clay took a long drink of the water George brought him and allowed he felt some better. "Harley, why don't you just lend me that mule? I'll go after him myself."

Thomas Begay eyed his nephew and spoke before Harley had a chance. "Billy, that mule's pretty green. Harley's the only one that's rode him so far and mules are particular who they take up with." He paused and tried to put the next thing as delicately as possible. "Harley's well known around here as a tracker…and you're not. That boy's got a pretty good jump on you and in the end I'm thinking it's going to come down to tracking…maybe some pretty fancy tracking at that. You better just let Harley handle it. If that boy can be caught Harley will catch him. You're lucky he's offered to do it for you Billy. Danny Hat's got clan all over down there in the canyons. He could just as easy get away clean if you're` not careful." This was all Thomas Begay could think of to discourage his nephew from an undertaking he thought might turn out badly.

Thomas was aware Harley's main motivation was likely just looking out for Danny Hat, who he considered harmless despite the man's troublesome ways. Probably, Harley figured it was the least he could do for Danny's people, who for the most part, were good folks, including Danny's sister who Harley had once been sweet on when they were kids. Thomas often wondered if Harley hadn't looked the girl up, now that his wife Anita had been gone over a year. Luanne wasn't married at the moment, and he'd heard she had a good job checking at the Co-Op. Maybe that's who Harley was thinking about. Luanne Keyoni was a little wild to some people's notion, but maybe that was what Harley needed.

Billy Red Clay sighed, chewed his lower lip and looked from Harley to Thomas. He knew his uncle was right but he, too, suspected Harley's motives. In the end the policeman, deciding he had no real choice, reluctantly nodded agreement, then reached into his patrol unit to raise dispatch on the radio. He figured to have another unit sent in from below just in case. If Danny Hat got by Harley somehow, they might still be able to pick him up down-canyon.

Harley Ponyboy tightened the mule's cinch a second time knowing the animal's tendency to hold a deep breath when first saddled. Harley would have thought less of him if he hadn't. Mules are always looking out for themselves and that's the thing he liked best about this one. He rocked the saddle back and forth and put some weight in the stirrup a couple of times before swinging aboard. The mule, with the re-tightening of the cinch stood flat-footed, possibly wondering if this would be a good time to buck…but he didn't on account it was Harley.

When he turned the mule toward the Navajo policeman Harley held up a finger. "You might let Charlie Yazzie know what's going on. I expect that boy out there might be needing some legal advice— I've heard them FBIs will bully a person when they can."

Billy Red Clay gave the little man a blank stare, then started to say something in the agency's defense but then decided otherwise and held his tongue. "I'll do that Harley." He knew Senior FBI Agent Eldon Mayfield wouldn't be pleased to have Charlie Yazzie involved in his business, and might even blame him for it. That could be a little worrisome, and possibly jeopardize his new position as Liaison Officer. On the other hand, he and Charlie Yazzie had always gotten on well—tribal police depended on Legal Services for all manner of information. *Yes, there was the chance this could get a little sticky.*

After they watched Harley Ponyboy edge the mule off into the draw, Professor Custer took it upon himself to enlighten the tribal policeman regarding the significance of the salvage operation in progress. George didn't like the term "salvage" but knew that was what they were doing. He pointed out various features of the stone dwellings and was a little disappointed when the law officer showed only polite interest. But before returning to his tent and the never-ending paperwork, George Custer also asked Billy to have Charlie Yazzie get in touch.

After the professor made his way back up the hill, Thomas Begay stayed on, talking to his nephew and as they waited, they wondered again what might have come over Danny Hat to make him act as he did.

Billy Red Clay again ventured the opinion, "The boy didn't seem 'right' somehow."

Even after talk turned to other matters, family mostly, a strange foreboding came over Thomas each time his thoughts turned to Harley Ponyboy. As the afternoon wore on he couldn't shake the feeling the little man had run into trouble. He and Harley had been friends for a long time and were more or less attuned to one another's thinking. He was still mulling over the possibilities when he spied Harley and his mule across the canyon and heading their way at a fast clip.

When Harley finally urged the mule up out of the draw it was plain, even from a distance that he had failed to bring in the fugitive. Thomas knew his friend to be a pit-bull when once on a scent and was one who didn't let go of a thing until he had given it a good shake. He was more than a little surprised, then, to see him come in empty handed. As the little man drew closer it was clear he had not only been hard on himself, but on the mule as well. The animal was lathered and carried his head low, ears flat out to either side in that pitiable state of dejection only a mule can pull off with any degree of credibility. Even the tribal policeman seemed taken aback to see Harley return so soon...and without the fugitive Danny Hat. Neither Thomas, nor the policeman called out to the rider; only watched quietly as Harley rode right up to the patrol unit and looked down at Billy Red Clay. Even then he didn't speak, or look directly at the young officer.

Billy frowned. "You didn't get him?"

"I didn't have to."

Billy squinted his one good eye and tried to maintain his composure, "Why not?"

Harley looked away for a moment and bit his lower lip. "Something already got him Billy. He's dead."

"Dead?" Billy Red Clay was stunned and for a moment unable to speak. When he did finally answer he stammered, "What happened to him?"

Harley could barely form the words. "Damned if I could tell." He didn't like thinking about Danny now. His views on death were traditional to say the least, and the less he thought about it the better. The mule was getting antsy, he was thirsty and wanted a drink and his dinner; he knew he had earned it.

Thomas Begay stepped up to take hold of the bridle. "Where did you find him Harley? You haven't been gone more'n a few hours."

"Danny only made it three or four miles from where we last saw him…maybe a little more." Harley got a faraway look in his eyes, as though he still couldn't believe what he had seen. "…Just sitting there against a juniper, hands folded in his lap, still had the cuffs on and all. But he's dead all right. I didn't have to touch him to see that…flies were already working him. I figured the Feds wouldn't want anyone mucking things up so I didn't go any closer. I couldn't see a mark on that boy. Whatever killed him didn't leave any sign. I backed out and cut a couple of circles way out around, but couldn't come up with anything ta speak of, no tracks or nothin'." Harley shot Thomas Begay an odd look, which Thomas took to mean there might be more to it than Harley was reporting.

Harley swung down off the mule, untied the still full water bottle, took a long slow swallow, and then wet his kerchief and began wiping his neck and face with it. "There's an old four-wheel drive track coming in from the lower canyon, almost up to where he's sitting." Harley mentioned this with the hope Billy Red Clay would have someone come in from that direction to retrieve the body, and not require any further involvement on his part. "There really isn't any good way in from up here Billy," he insisted. "Unless you want to pack him out horseback." The policeman stayed staring at the ground for a moment, shook his head finally, and turned back to the radio. Things had gone downhill fast from the time he had first arrested Danny Hat. Billy Red Clay figured he might as well get in touch with Agent Mayfield and lay it all out for him. The FBI man wouldn't be happy with this turn of events, but Billy knew he would definitely want to be in on the recovery. He would have to bring along his forensic people of course; that would mean a long wait. Farmington wasn't far as the crow flies but it was a circuitous route to the lower end of that canyon. This could well turn into an all-nighter, and given the circumstances, Eldon Mayfield was not someone he was eager to spend the night with.

After Harley unsaddled and watered the mule he staked him out on a patch of grass then came back to wait for Billy Red Clay to finish his conversation. Dispatch was having a little trouble making him out, and unable to pinpoint the subject's location on their topo maps. Navajo are soft talkers; a few thousand years of relative quiet had pretty much eliminated the need for loud talk. Billy raised his voice to a near shout, thinking that might help...and it did.

When Harley looked over at him, Thomas Begay glanced back, nodded, and headed up the hill to inform the professor of the news. He would talk to Harley later, but he had a pretty good idea what was on his mind. While Harley hadn't touched the body, he had been there soon enough that he might now perceive himself at risk, especially since there was no apparent cause of death. It could have been some sort of witchery and Danny Hat's *chindi* might still have been hanging around. Thomas knew Harley would feel vulnerable enough to be thinking of a singer. He would have felt much the same himself; he and Harley were of a like mind when it came to dead people.

Billy Red Clay eventually wound up his business on the two-way, and after taking down Harley Ponyboy's statement and getting his signature, left to meet with a tribal unit at the turnoff. They would most likely have to wait there for the feds, as he doubted Senior Agent Mayfield or his people could find the place without someone being there to show them the way.

Billy once thought being Liaison Officer between Tribal and the FBI a good career move, but was beginning to think maybe that was a mistake. He *was* off regular patrol duty and *did* have the new car, but the added worries that came with the job, and dealing with Eldon Mayfield, might be more than he bargained for. Billy originally thought the agent a more or less reasonable man despite being from New York city, but of late things were taking another direction altogether and he was not sure where that might eventually lead. Maybe Charlie Yazzie had been right when he said Eldon would never fit in on the reservation. Billy did sometimes hope Jr. Agent Fred Smith out of the Albuquerque office might eventually succeed to the position. There had been talk of it, and he knew Eldon would jump at the chance to quit the reservation and return to what he often referred to as civilization. Fred Smith on the other hand was originally from the Four Corners, still had family around Bloomfield, and had let it be known he would welcome the opportunity to return. In his opinion it would be a step up for the younger FBI man. Billy liked Fred and knew Charlie Yazzie did as well. The policeman hoped his office might someday be able to work with the Bureau on a more equal basis.

2

1075 A.D.

The Journey

In the chill of predawn the boy moved to the edge of the alcove, peered into the shadowed canyon, and sorted through the jumble of thoughts and dreams from the night before. Today things would be different. Today they would start laying walls for his house. He was no longer a boy…but not yet a man. That would come when he took a woman. She must be of another clan, probably from a distant settlement, and likely, a person he had never seen before. Finding her wouldn't be easy. These were perilous times—people were suspicious and wary of strangers.

These were the thoughts that troubled the boy, making him feel unsure and a bit afraid.

~~~~~~

The boy's clan had been first among those to leave the great town to the south. Now the outlands were sprinkled with small settlements, sometimes only two or three families, or a single clan. Those settling at the farthest reaches found trouble—reports of wild bands from the north harassing those not on their guard; women and children stolen from the fields and such crops that survived the drought raided in the night.

There had been a time when those wandering hunters were trading partners, exchanging hides and dried meat for corn and beans. Now game was scarce, and there was little left to trade on either side. Isolated groups of their own kind were becoming desperate too, covetous of their more prosperous neighbors. Those who had nothing began to prey upon those who had even a little.

The elders thought it only a matter of time before the fiercest of these people gathered in raiding parties and threatened the entire region. The boy's clan was few in number, alone in a hostile land, and while it was of their own doing he sometimes wondered if the elders had made the right decision. Leaving the safety of the larger town would have been a risky move even in good times.

The elders in their defense, cited the strange new ideas filtering in from beyond the great southern desert, where there were said to be noble civilizations with peculiar customs, and even more powerful Gods. First there were only a few traders and they brought wondrous things, tiny copper bells, brightly colored feathers, and iridescent shell ornaments to dazzle the eye. It was only later their holy men appeared, taller more imperious beings who implied their Gods had the power to bring rain. These strangers were fortunate to appear when they did—the rains did return for a time, and the newcomers were quick to take credit. Great buildings were begun, and demands upon the people grew more strident as a new class developed. Their grip on the people tightened, and their followers, became many.

Over time, clan elders, including his own father, came to consider these interlopers and their Gods dangerous, and likely to anger the Deities of their ancestors. Turmoil and unrest divided the people as never before—old customs were scorned and the elders challenged at every turn. Their world grew more complicated. The boy's own sister was a target followers of the new order cast suspicious glances her way, frowned into their feather blankets, and exchanged knowing looks. *The holy men would have had such individuals abandoned... or worse.* In the end, the elders were forced to make a life-changing decision. Now, *his* people were the outliers.

From the dwelling's open doorway there came whimpering, all the more pitiful in that lonely time before dawn. The girl awaited the sun and the warmth of that life-giving orb; soon she would call to be brought outside, into the warmth, hoping to gain some small respite from the pain. After her accident, his mother would rub each injured limb, stretching each one in turn, praying some lasting good might come of it. Now, only he and his father were left to care for the girl. *Still she hung on, season after season, year after year, her condition growing ever worse...and where would they be then? The girl's powers were evident early on and she now held their future in her hands.*

The passing of thirty-nine winters had left his father already old. It was a hard life in the canyons, requiring constant work. The work took its toll, and his wife's death only doubled the burden. Grit from the grinding stones wore down his teeth leaving them vulnerable to sugars in the corn they so desperately depended on. Bad teeth brought illness and aged a person beyond their years. The wild game had been hunted out, and native plants produced only sporadically. With less and less food of any sort, the people grew weak and unable to harvest resources in more distant areas. The boy was aware his father ate less now, leaving more for them. The old man no longer worried about putting something aside for winter.

The rains had been late again. The he-rains should already be pushing their way up from the south. In the *kiva* the elders held the ceremonies, sang the secret songs and smoked their cone-shaped clay pipes, sending little rain clouds of smoke to now heedless Gods…who paid them no mind. In the fields above the canyon rim the corn and beans soon exhausted what little groundwater filtered down from meager winter snows. Squash blossoms languished in the heat of the afternoon and withered on the vine.

When first arrived they had immediately begun repairs to washed out dams and ditches left by those who came before. But the boy's people were too few, and the repairs too late. Those first builders lived openly, on the flats above the canyon, just next to their fields. In those better times hunger had not yet forced the wild bands to go scavenging. Now, even *should* the rains come, there was little chance the dams would catch enough to revive the crops. There now seemed little hope for more than a token harvest. Winter winds would soon howl through the canyons, pushing the specter of starvation before them.

These were the things the boy was thinking there in the shelter of the cliff, awaiting dawn on the day he was to start his new rooms.

As the sun began fingering its way under the rim a quiet call from the old man interrupted the boy's thoughts; the voice from the doorway summoned him to help with his sister.

Coming into the light the girl closed her eyes in pleasure and reached with thin and trembling arms toward the warmth. Her tattered rabbit fur cloak was drawn close about her shoulders, and she luxuriated in the healing rays.

His sister had not taken a single step since the accident and of late required even more dedicated care and attention. Despite her discomfort she remained pleasant and generally of a good humor. When pain did not cloud her mind, she had visions and saw things others couldn't. After a time, even the elders came to inquire after her health, fetched her potions they said might help, then slyly and in roundabout ways, sought her council. There were those among them who believed she could foresee the future and brought little gifts of food, thinking hope more important than the growing hunger in their bellies.

The cliff swallows twittered in mud nests, flitting this way and that, diving in long graceful swoops to the canyon depths—only to rise again on the lifting currents. The girl's face brightened at the sight of them. She nodded knowingly to her brother and murmured, "That is how I will fly one day," and smiled as she watched the little creatures soar upon the breeze.

3

The Tecolote

When he took the call from tribal, Charlie Yazzie had other things on his mind; it took him nearly a minute to grasp the full gist of the message. Navajo Police dispatcher Mildred Dahozy was the last person he wanted to talk to, especially today. The woman had been a longtime friend of his grandmother's and a known talker when she cornered someone she thought obligated to listen. Charlie knew he was in for a long siege, and one with little hope getting a word in edgewise. Mildred inquired after the health of everyone in his family, including his Aunt Annie Eagletree, who she had been on the outs with for more than fifteen years, and still never referred to by name.

Finally, the Greasewood Clan woman got around to giving him a communication from Billy Red Clay. The message itself, took only a few seconds: "Call me ASAP – Billy." It took Mildred several minutes more, however, to close out her own ideas regarding what the message might reference. She pondered aloud what Billy might actually have intended, and what Charlie should do about it—none of which, as it turned out, bore any resemblance to what the message actually involved or required of him.

Charlie looked at the clock above the office door and frowned—thirty minutes left in a slow Friday afternoon. Earlier, his wife Sue was adamant he should get home on time for a change. She told him she had a leg of lamb in the oven old man Paul T'Sosi had dropped by fresh killed, only hours before. She invited the old singer to stay for supper as was polite, Paul, she said, was at that moment out weeding her garden, which he insisted was payment in advance for the supper. Though he had supplied the main course himself, he thought that beside the point. The old man was a great favorite of the Yazzie's and both knew he held their son Joseph Wiley in high regard. Paul was often heard to say he thought the boy might have powers, and was like a grandson to him.

Charlie's mouth watered at the thought of the lamb. Sue's cooking skills had improved over the last year and lamb was on her good list. He thought he would at least like to have his dinner before calling Billy Red Clay. The policeman didn't often require his help, and when he did it was generally not a trivial matter. That bothered him. The Legal Services investigator sat drumming his fingers on the edge of the desk as he watched the clock. Finally, he gave in and dialed the switchboard to have the operator patch him through tribal to Billy Red Clay's unit.

Billy's first words were an apology. "I'm sorry as hell about this Charlie...I know you're going home in a few minutes..." The policeman's radio crackled in and out and the two chewed up the final twenty minutes of Charlie's Friday afternoon trying to understand one another. Between periods of static Billy did his best to cover all that had taken place at Professor Custer's salvage site, and several times made it clear that both Harley Ponyboy, and Dr. Custer, had requested Charlie contact them as soon as possible.

After he finished with Billy Red Clay, Charlie called Sue to let her know he would be home on time, and to have her tell Paul T'Sosi he might want to stay over that night—there could be work for him out at the dig in the morning. On the short drive home reassessing the report in his mind took nearly as long as the original conversation. And in the final analysis left just as much to conjecture.

Charlie was glad to have the old singer accompany him. Paul had been helping out at the professor's office in Farmington, mostly just labeling specimens for shipment, but in his younger days had worked on several major excavations. Those excavations included portions of the Aztec Ruins along the Animas River, and not so far from the professor's current project. The man was well acquainted with basic excavating procedure and liked nothing better than joining the regular crew from time to time. Paul's health had suffered these last months however, leaving him unable to do as much as he would have liked. Charlie knew Paul would enjoy a trip to the dig and getting his hands dirty. The old man especially liked overseeing the work of his son-in-law Thomas Begay, and was never shy about speaking his mind when he saw something amiss in Thomas's efforts.

Charlie knew for certain Harley Ponyboy would be spending a restless night. Both Harley and Thomas were sticklers for cleansing rituals should they think something evil had a bead on them. Harley came from a very traditional clan, one that saw little need of him attending government school. The boy's deep-seated belief in all manner of magic, witches and other *Yeenaaldiooshii* remained unaffected by what little white schooling he had been subjected to. Charlie, on the other hand, had come away from university with a growing skepticism of many of the old ways, and especially struggled to hold his tongue in talk regarding the supernatural. He knew those beliefs ran deep in his people, and attempting to change that thinking was generally unproductive.

That night when supper was finished, Sue received several compliments on the meal and felt pleased. Later, when a sleepy but protesting, Joseph Wiley was trundled off to bed the men were left alone with their coffee. While Charlie was not clear on many of the details, he attempted to sound Paul out on the Danny Hat affair. The old man listened attentively and only occasionally did he ask a question. From what he was hearing Paul figured he would be performing at least one cleansing ceremony the next day. His son-in-law, Thomas Begay, while not quite as traditional as Harley Ponyboy, was not one to let a virtually free healing opportunity pass. Who knew what good might come of such a thing, especially when one considered Thomas's occasional departures from the Beauty Way. Harley would get the standard discount allotted to close friends and distant family. Thomas, on the other hand, was generally charged little or nothing as Paul had given up on collecting from his son-in-law. In Thomas's mind his marriage to the singer's daughter assured him of the same free spiritual insurance as any other member of the family. He was well aware Paul wouldn't allow any threat to go unchallenged when it came to home and family.

To be fair, Thomas did perform those small favors involving those things the old singer was no longer capable of doing for himself, including driving him around to consult with those in need of his services. In the beginning Paul had not been a great fan of his new son-in-law, but when Thomas quit drinking and became self-supporting to the point of adding to the family economy, a truce was called and the two gradually came to tolerate one another. Thomas's natural charm coupled with the *Dinés'* cultural affinity for family had eventually won the old man over.

Charlie and Paul T'Sosi agreed to leave for the dig at first light with the general thought in mind of a quick trip. Charlie was aware these little excursions often turned out to take a good bit longer than planned. Sue also knew this to be true, and followed their preparations and promise of a quick return with a jaundiced eye. She cuddled her young son at the breakfast table, feeding him cereal, and thinking unkind thoughts of the warrior-like bond still apparent among Navajo men who came together in a like cause. Many shades of the old ways still thrive on the *Dinétah*, even among those who professed otherwise.

~~~~~~~

Charlie Yazzie followed as the old singer slowly made his way up from the roadstead, stopping only briefly at the professor's horse trailer to appraise Harley's mule. The animal had recovered from his previous day's trials and was busily engaged in deciphering the twists and turns of the knot that held him.

Paul arched his eyebrows at Jake, his tone implying some hidden flaw, "So, *this* is Harley's new mule?"

"That's him." Charlie nodded and smiled. "You know Harley—he likes a challenge."

The old man sniffed, watched a few seconds longer before saying, "That mule's going to figure out that knot before lunchtime. It will be interesting to see how hard he is to catch, once he's had a little taste of freedom."

Upon being welcomed into the cook tent by Professor Custer the newcomers shook hands all around. Everyone was well acquainted, and despite the circumstances seemed pleased at the opportunity to get together. The *Diné* arranged themselves around the table, taking their places at the far end, away from the collection of maps and charts the professor had been poring over. The archaeologist took it upon himself to serve coffee from a still warm pot and placed a package of cookies in the center of the table. He was well versed in Navajo social niceties and felt it important to follow them when possible.

Dr. Custer looked first to the old singer, "Paul, I suppose you've come to help Harley with his little predicament?" And then gave Thomas a calculating look. "Thomas here, somehow believes himself at risk as well...some sort of evil flying off of Harley and hooking onto him no doubt."

Thomas smiled, nodded affably, and offered no defense, saying, "Now Doc, a little spiritual support can't do any harm. It will only take an hour or so and will assure me and Harley of a guaranteed dose of good *hozo*."

Paul T'Sosi frowned at Professor Custer and set his jaw. "There's more to it than that George. It's not just about Danny Hat; there is also the run-in with the highway workers and the bad feelings that came from that. All these things can affect these boys' *hozo*, and cause them to fall out of step with their people." He looked at the two men in question and his eyes came to rest on Thomas. "These two have always been close—what affects the *hozoji* of one could rub off on the other."

Professor Custer wearily shook his head and considered. "Well, it's Saturday and while I did say we wouldn't be taking any time off until we get ahead of the road crew... I guess we have to do what we have to do." He smiled weakly and nodded at the pair. "I suppose an hour or so won't make much difference." George knew there would be very little work accomplished until this *chindi* thing was taken care of, and in the end both men would have to be convinced of the cure.

Harley beamed and clapped the professor on the back. "That's the spirit Doc. A little religion never hurt no one."

Paul T'Sosi nodded, satisfied, then rose from his chair and followed the two afflicted parties outside to begin preparations for the ritual. Charlie Yazzie rose from his own chair, lifted an eyebrow at the professor and moved to the tent door. He couldn't help remembering how his grandfather told him as a child that *Ma'iitsoh*, the Navajo wolf, would be waiting for him if he disrespected his elders. Such fears still came to him occasionally, in his dreams, but no one knew.

Dr. Custer and Charlie watched from a distance as the other three gathered materials to build a sweat lodge. Thomas and Harley Ponyboy had already found most of what was needed the night before, requisitioning a small tarp from the pile of supplies for the salvage operation. It wasn't long before the sweat lodge was erected, and a stone fire ring laid just outside the door, water and a dipper was put at hand just inside. Thomas started the fire, watching carefully as Harley pushed the stones closer to the blaze before adding more split cedar to cover the stones. Paul T'Sosi inspected everything with a critical eye and pronounced it workable. When the stones became a shade of gray-hot Thomas used a shovel to fill a bucket, then with a forked stick through the bail, placed the container in the center of the lodge.

It was a small lodge, not tall enough for the three men to stand upright; before entering they stripped themselves of outer clothing. Paul T'Sosi carried a small bundle of green sage, his pollen bag, and a gourd rattle. Thomas laid the shovel handle just under the flap in case things went into overtime and more heated stones were needed. Thomas knew this would be unlikely; his father-in-law would direct the main brunt of the cure to Harley Ponyboy as he was the one most in need, and the one who would be paying in actual cash.

It was already hot outside; Charlie couldn't imagine what the temperature was inside the lodge. Paul T'Sosi was the last to enter. Professor Custer had earlier gone so far as to suggest to Thomas the old man might be too frail for the cruel heat of the lodge, and then ventured the opinion the singer might be just as effective singing the chants and calling out the exhortations from outside where it was cooler.

Paul snorted at this, brushed it aside, and wouldn't hear of it. While it was not uncommon for a person in desperate circumstance to perform the ceremony alone and without benefit of a singer, most thought this risky and left much to go wrong. No, everyone knew it was best to have a trained *hataalii* for the praying, one who knew the proper sequence of the songs, when to use the sage, and offer the pollen. Only in this way could a cure be guaranteed and the entire effort not be wasted.

The professor and Charlie seated themselves on packing boxes outside the tent and looked on with guarded interest. Though both men had witnessed similar rituals a number of times, they agreed no two of the rites had been performed exactly the same. Charlie thought this might be because the perceived illnesses were so varied. Few Navajo beliefs or customs are set in stone, and procedures often depend on both the affliction, and the *singer's* best guess of how strong a cure is needed to overcome it. Some Hataalii become adept at judging these things, and become quite popular, commanding impressive prices for their services. Others, not so talented, may scrape along their entire careers with only a few patients, never really attaining the reputation they once aspired to. Paul T'Sosi had come late to the calling and without the avarice associated with those who sought a more material gain from their services. Paul charged only what he thought his patients could afford and thus was usually required to accept at least part of his fee in produce, sheep, and like goods.

Dr. Custer had known Charlie Yazzie in his earliest days at university, and had watched the boy's belief in traditional superstition and all manner of witchcraft wane considerably over the years. George had seen this with other Indian students as well. He wondered if hidden doubt and confusion might still shadow Charlie's *hozo*—that state of well being that makes a *Diné* one with his people and allows him to *walk in beauty*.

Charlie watched, and despite his years of doubt, began to feel a sense of peace and serenity fall over him. He listened, nearly mesmerized, to the chants and rhythmic rattle of the gourd, it was hypnotic, and as the heady essence of sage and piñon wafted from the lodge he wondered if he was coming under some random reawakening of spirit, something from his childhood perhaps—a feeling he might never again experience or even be able to define.

George Custer eyed his former student and could see the ceremony, simple though it was, had obviously touched him. There were reasons the *Diné* believed what they did about healing and that anyone who attended might take away a portion of good for themselves. George found the ceremony interesting, but was without the genetic or cultural connection to allow any such effect.

As Paul T'Sosi brought the healing to a close it took Charlie a few moments to regain a sense of time and place. He and the professor stood for a moment each with his own thoughts before moving inside to allow Paul T'Sosi and his two patients some privacy to dress.

Inside the tent, George hesitated to break the lingering effect of the ceremony but was anxious to hear the latest in the Danny Hat affair. "What have you heard from the FBI...about Danny Hat I mean? Have they found what killed him?" The professor had held off bringing the subject up until after the cleansing.

Charlie paused his train of thought and directed a glance out the tent flap where he saw Harley and Thomas reclaiming their clothes from the stack of firewood. He turned to the professor and answered, "No, nothing official...should be only three or four days before the coroner's report comes back though. The chief medical officer is waiting on results from the lab in Albuquerque." He looked again toward the tent opening as the flaps fluttered in a fresh breeze. "Billy Red Clay, of course, didn't stay for the preliminary examination." Charlie smiled as he continued. "He said dead people don't really bother him so much anymore, but admits he's still a little leery and tries to avoid them when possible." He and the professor both smiled and Charlie held up a quantifying finger. "He did say the medical examiner told him there were no signs of external trauma apparent on the body. Oddly enough the doctor suspected Danny's heart might have given out, a stroke maybe, brought on by the heat and running. He was badly dehydrated according to the doc." Once again Charlie eased over to the tent flaps and peered out to make sure no one was near. "I wouldn't say anything about this to the others George—Danny Hat's dying without visible cause might spell witchery. Even though Harley and Thomas should now feel well protected in that regard, you just never know." The Legal Services Investigator paused and looked in the direction of the sweat lodge, Harley was taking down. "At least now their minds will be eased enough to go on with their work."

Paul and the others finally came to the tent and drank copious amounts of water from the barrel beside the door, after which the two patients declared themselves cured and ready to return to the project. Neither of the two men referred to the ceremony or made further inquiry into the matter of Danny Hat. They would try not to think of him in the future.

A few minutes later Charlie grinned, looked up from one of the professor's reports he was reading and motioned George Custer from his grid charts. Old man Paul T'Sosi had taken up a shovel and was following the other two to the kiva they had been excavating. He appeared none the worse for his time in the sweat lodge and, in fact, had a spring in his step they hadn't noticed before.

"Do you think he's up to using that shovel?" Professor Custer whispered.

"Well, he must think he is," Charlie said, "I suppose that's a good indicator. He's a tough old bird and this might be the best thing for him." He then took up a shovel himself and headed toward the excavation.

Charlie Yazzie as an undergraduate had been one of Custer's most promising students; the professor often spoke of his intuitive bent for archaeology. In later years he would go so far as to remark it had been a mistake for Charlie to switch his major to Law. Privately Dr. Custer still thought so, though he now agreed Charlie had proven himself in his chosen field as well.

When they reached the shade of the alcove they found Harley Ponyboy and Thomas Begay already hard at work. Paul, with a trowel and screen, sifted portions of a fill area made up of household middins he found interesting he judged interesting only by the color and texture of the deposit. None of the men needed instruction in correct procedure. This was salvage archaeology, more of a recovery effort than anything else and not to be confused with the concise and time-consuming investigation of a more scientific probe. Still, Charlie knew salvage people were often qualified and experienced workers picked to do the best job possible in the time available. Salvage projects were ones in imminent danger of being destroyed, drowned, or otherwise eliminated from their place in recorded history. Whatever can be cataloged and saved is thought all to the good. Professor Custer knew in the not so distant past he would have been hard pressed to find Navajo who would even consider working in these ruins. While that was still sometimes the case, much had changed over the years and many of the rangers and other workmen in the Reservation's National Parks and Monuments were now Indian.

While this particular little Anasazi site was not thought to be in immediate peril, new state guidelines decreed a qualified person should at least have a cursory look. In the initial surveys Dr. Custer first thought this site little different from those further up the canyon. Though it was clear the others were from a slightly earlier time, this is the one that aroused the professor's curiosity. Recent looting of the upper mesa top ruins had been a factor in that decision. There had been incursions so systematic and thorough as to leave the sites with very little of scientific value. Beyond a quick survey and photo documentation of those looted sites, Custer thought his time better spent on this more protected and less spoiled cluster of dwellings. Time was short and state funding unreliable at best. He knew the highway department was champing at the bit, petitioning higher-ups to cancel the salvage project altogether.

In its little alcove below the rim, the defensive nature of the site had immediately attracted the archaeologist's attention; further investigation only heightened his interest. The masonry was classic Chaco and he hoped it might provide some crucial link to the scattered northward resettlement following the great towns' "golden age."

The site was only ten or twelve ground floor apartments and less than half that in second story rooms—with a scattering of storage bins here and there among the cracks and fissures. There was a small *kiva* in the forefront of the dwellings requiring an outer retaining wall to be built, with rock and dirt fill still supporting the chambers lower walls.

A tiny round tower sat atop the end room, just at the entry to the alcove, an unusual feature to say the least. Custer suspected it was a lookout that might afford easier surveillance of the lower trail that edged across the face of the cliff. To his mind it was yet another indicator of a period when increased security was thought necessary. There had been just the one single-file access to the cliff-side apartments, further evidence of the turmoil brought about by a dark period of climate change, change so severe as to prove the beginning of the end for these ancient people. Dr. Custer had a special interest in this drastic change and the great drought it brought with it, especially in regard to these small outlier groups. He surmised no more than twenty-five or thirty people might have made their home in this village at any one time, and possibly for only one or two generations.

Thomas Begay and Harley Ponyboy had become so proficient in their work they now required little overseeing. The professor had spent a good bit of time digging alongside them and they were apt students. They learned to hurry through the fill, fallen rubble of the walls, and debris of roofing material, to concentrate their main efforts at base level—that's where the more important finds were likely to be made.

Charlie had just picked what he thought might be a productive spot inside the grid marked for the day's investigation when the professor appeared with a sheaf of papers in hand and called him to follow. The archaeologist pointed to the last room in the little complex—the room with the small second-floor tower guarding the narrow ledge beyond the entry.

George Custer began by saying, "There can be little doubt the lower path up to the dwellings once followed a very narrow ledge, along the face of that cliff, one easily defended should one remain alert and have a pile of stones at their disposal."

"That end room," the professor said, pointing, "would have been the first line of defense against intruders, and whoever lived in that room would have had the duty of alerting the others and repelling enemies until help arrived." The professor hesitated then seemed to consider further. "There does seem to have been some sort of stone barrier at the narrowest section of trail. Further out there is the main trail up to the top and the fields. "It makes a person wonder what kind of people it took to work… or even survive under these conditions." He shook his head as though to clear those thoughts. "There had to have been happy times I'm sure, but always there seems to have been an undercurrent of desperation in these people and their life here in the canyons." The professor's face brightened. "I have roughly dated this site to those years before a later, and more severe drought, forced the great migration out of this area and it is one of the few small sites in the canyon to plainly show the Chaco influence. This might possibly have been an offshoot of the Chacoan phase at Aztec Ruins National Monument."

Charlie nodded, agreeing with the professor's basic assessment. He felt the old urge to know more about this particular little band of people and how they lived. He gazed past the broken walls and he too, silently wondered. *What incredible hardships they must have endured during those times. The stories these walls could tell...*

Once again the two men became teacher and student, and together fell to clearing rubble and chatting as they had so often in the past.

It was late afternoon when Thomas Begay looked up from his work and saw a tribal police unit easing its way down the rough grade that was to become part of the new highway. He poked Harley, and pointed. "Look who's back. My nephew must think he needs to keep an eye on us up here." Thomas stayed leaning on his shovel, watching as the unit came to a stop and the officer stepped down and looked around the staging area.

Harley barely raised his head and gave no more than a quick glance toward the road. In a muffled voice he said, "I think I might be on ta something here," then pulled down his bandanna and tapped the point of his shovel against a large flat stone—there was a hollow clunk. Bending closer he gave it another light tap...something definitely sounded different.

Thomas paid no attention, concentrating instead on his nephew down below then decided. "Billy looks a little put out, if you know what I mean." He then waved to catch his nephew's attention and whistled toward the others at their digging, thinking they had missed the sound of the car's approach. When still no one took notice he shouted and waved an arm in their direction.

Charlie Yazzie's head popped out of a doorway; he looked about, thinking the professor might have called from across the site. George and old man Paul T'Sosi had been digging a test hole last he saw of them. Thomas waved again then pointed; finally Charlie caught sight of Officer Billy Red Clay and understood.

Thomas poked Harley who was still bent over his shovel, reluctant to leave off his investigation. "Something's going on, little man. You can mess with that rock later."

Harley muttered, "This thing looks like it might really be somethin' ...maybe I better..."

"I guess whatever it is will keep Harley. It's been there a thousand years. I doubt it's going anywhere in the next few minutes. It would be rude for you to ignore my nephew. He's always liked you."

Harley sighed, laid down his shovel and he and Thomas moved to join the others picking their way to meet the tribal policeman. Billy was waving a piece of paper and seemed anxious to show it to someone. Everyone came together at about the same time, though Harley, glancing back at the *kiva*, had lagged a little behind.

The policeman stopped to catch his breath and let them come closer. Charlie was first there and was surprised to see a rather sinister look on Billy's placid features. *Maybe it was the black, swollen eye—that was new.* He paused mid-step, hesitant, waiting for the policeman to speak.

Billy cleared his throat and seemed to be having trouble getting the words out. "Sue told me you would be up here." He hooked a thumb over his shoulder. "That supervisor...foreman, up at the road construction filed a complaint against me." His voice was ragged, edged with emotion, and nearly a growl. "That bastard Karl Hoffman claims I threatened him with violence...said we were on Ute land, and I had no authority there."

Charlie held up a hand. "What?" and then took the paper the lawman held. "Hold on a minute Billy." Charlie had already heard about the confrontation with the road foreman, but this sounded like the situation might be escalating. After reading the complaint he asked, "Did you go by the road camp and talk to the guy?" He thought that might be something Billy Red Clay would do—the lawman was not one to mince words, or back off a delicate situation.

Billy made a visible effort to speak more clearly and his next words were calm and measured. "I did go up there, but the maintenance man was the only one around; the dozer was off in the ditch and on its side. When I asked about Karl Hoffman, the guy said there had been an accident and the others had taken him to the hospital in Farmington." Billy frowned and looked back up the hill toward the road camp. "I asked him why they hadn't called for an ambulance, and he looked at me kind of funny... said they didn't think Karl would last long enough for the ambulance to get out here and back."

Thomas interrupted his nephew, "It sounds to me like it was probably a good thing those road boys was gone, you might have made things a whole lot worse going up there." He narrowed his eyes at the younger man. "There was plenty of people heard what took place at our little run-in with Karl Hoffman. I doubt there'll be any problem once that's set straight."

"Right now, Uncle," Billy said quietly, "The 'complaint' is not what I'm worried about. I just called dispatch on the two-way and had them patch me through to the hospital." Here Billy Red Clay turned to look out across the canyon and for a moment seemed to have trouble finding his voice.

"So how is he Billy?" Charlie was getting a bad feeling about this.

The policeman didn't bother to turn around when he answered. "He's dead Charlie; the attending physician said he had been shot off that dozer. It was no accident." Complete silence enveloped the little group and hung like a shroud.

No one dared look at anyone else, and Thomas put a hand on his nephew's shoulder to slowly turn him around. "Where were *you* during that time he was shot *Shiye'?*" Thomas used the Navajo word meaning 'nephew' and looked directly at him when he said it.

Billy's eyes did not meet those of his uncle. "I don't know for sure but I couldn't have been very far. The man said they had left with Hoffman only about twenty minutes before I pulled up."

"You didn't pass them on their way out?" Charlie thought things might be taking yet another turn for the worse.

"No," Billy said, almost in a whisper. "No one passed me going out that I saw."

Now Harley Ponyboy edged up to Charlie and spoke in a low voice, "There is that old cut-across this side of Rock Stands Up. It's rough but people still use it...saves about ten miles for those who know about it."

Thomas nodded, "I've been that way...could be those boys used it to save time. Seems I heard they graded it recently for those trucks coming in with heavy equipment. They wouldn't have to go over the pass that way neither; that pass is a pretty good pull for the big equipment haulers." Everyone could see the implication of proximity and motive, but nonetheless, wanted to show support for Billy Red Clay, and were eager to discount these things in the process. This Navajo policeman was family to Thomas, and by association, related to Paul T'Sosi as well. He was in fact well thought of by the entire group. No one wanted to see him wrongly accused.

Charlie, had known the young officer a long time, well before he was a policeman, and couldn't imagine him capable of such an act. "What did your Lieutenant say about the complaint Hoffman filed?"

"He said he wouldn't do anything until he talked to the Captain, but did say I wouldn't be suspended without a preliminary investigation—probably take a day or so."

It was then old man Paul T'Sosi moved up close to Billy and boldly asked, "Do you think you need a cleansing ceremony Grandson?"

Everyone knew what the old singer was really asking, including Billy, and he looked directly at him before answering. No, Paul, I don't need any ceremony. I didn't shoot Karl Hoffman."

Paul nodded, looked closely at the younger man before stepping back and seemed satisfied with the answer.

Charlie Yazzie paused and thought for a moment. "Billy, I expect this killing might cause your Captain to rethink his position on that suspension. I think it best everyone present at that little altercation sign a deposition stating exactly what was said. I'll need something I can present to Captain Beyale to head off any further damage from that complaint Hoffman filed. It might allow enough time for a proper investigation, one that could clear you of wrongdoing before any actual charges can be filed." Charlie's expression didn't change when he looked at Billy Red Clay and cautioned, "You being out here at the time of the shooting is going to look bad no matter what, but at least we'll have an arguing point when I talk to Captain Beyale." The Legal Services Investigator's voice grew more serious. "Doctors are required to report gunshot wounds immediately. I would imagine there is a police report being filed in Farmington as we speak."

As the men stood there, each with his own thoughts, the hoot of an owl drifted down from the ancient village. There was not a man among them that didn't know its implication. Even the white professor, knew the hoot of an owl in daylight was dreaded by these people and was considered a harbinger of evil. A creature that can see in the black of night has always been thought to have supernatural powers and a possible cohort of evil forces. Many fear hearing an owl even at night and feel sorry for its prey.

Harley's eyes were wide when he mouthed the Mexican name for an owl. *"Tecolote…"* Harley knew the old Navajo word for the great horned owl, *né'éshjaatsoh,* but avoided saying it for fear it might draw the bird's attention.

Thomas took his cue from Harley and he, too, looked worried, casting about for further signs of evil.

"I think we better call it a day, it's almost four o'clock anyway."

Harley chimed in, "That would be good, give that thing time to fly away."

This was the sort of talk that caused Charlie Yazzie to grimace and shake his head, even though he knew the same stigma was attached to the bird in many other cultures including most other Indian tribes…and a number of white ones as well. When at university a white boy from the mountains of North Carolina told him; should he hear the call of an owl in daylight, someone close was sure to die. Charlie had since thought of that boy many times and wondered at the way even educated people will often hang on to things they believed as a child.

4

1075 A.D.

Retribution

From the shade of a piñon pine the boy glanced up the back-trail and for the hundredth time checked to see that no one followed. They had come far... further than they first intended. But of the first two villages, one was not inclined to let go of either of the two available young women, as they were already promised. Either would have made a fine wife in his father's opinion. In the second settlement the only unmarried woman was older, and though of a suitable clan the boy thought her surly, ill natured, and kept a poor house. The boy's father, in a hurry to return home, was of the opinion a light beating might well cure her of those vices. Still the boy would not budge, saying the woman was also unattractive, and his father was forced to agree a beating would not help that.

~~~~~~

They had been three days on the trail with very little to eat; as the boy watched the old man he could see he was growing weak and tired and they were forced to rest and forage for food. But pickings were lean and both were hungry. The old man shook the branches of the piñon tree, gleaning the few nuts left in the pinecones. The first freeze had already come and gone in these high places and most of the cones had released their seeds. The ground squirrels and packrats made short work of them. If they had more time, the old man thought, they might seek out the nests of those creatures and take their caches. The hoard of a busy packrat could half-fill a storage bin and such windfalls were eagerly sought by the women and children of the village. Nothing they were aware of provided more nourishment for its size than the piñon nut.

The old man cast furtive glances at his son, noting how he continuously swept the horizons for movement, pausing only to study the trail ascending the ridge before them. He thought, *my son has the makings of a warrior...but it is farmers we need.* He knew the boy's mind was made up and could see he was determined to press on. The boy had always been of a stubborn nature and when once he set his mind to a thing he probably couldn't be argued out of it.

Twice they had seen scattered tracks, not the tracks of yucca fiber sandals such as their own, but of footwear made of animal hide. Nor were these the prints of just one or two people, but rather a group of seven or eight men—large men by the size of the tracks. They were heading in the same direction… toward the western village.

The old man bent close, and narrowed his eyes at the prints before finally admitting the obvious. "These are those wild people who live on meat and roam that country to the north. They will kill us if they can."

The boy nodded, knew it was true, but still was not swayed and asked, "How long ago?"

His father bent again and lifted the edges of the curly-grass, tested its resiliency where a moccasin had tread on it. "Two days I think, maybe more…it's been dry…so maybe more."

A chill ran down the boy's back and he viewed the ridge ahead in a different light. They had not counted on this, but had known from the start it was possible, and prepared as best they could. He carried a bow and a badger skin quiver of arrows. It had taken days to fashion the bow, then straighten and finish the arrows. The obsidian points cost him another three days work in his uncle's parched fields. Obsidian was not easy to come by, his uncle said. This piece had come in trade from the old town. The uncle was a master worker of flint and obsidian; each point was razor sharp and designed to penetrate deep and true. The uncle had also knapped a fine obsidian blade and hafted it with deer bone for a handle. This he gave the boy as a gift, saying he felt it his duty to provide something more suited for close quarters. It was that same uncle's wife who now looked after the boy's sister until they returned.

Already the time away was weighing on his father, who could only hope his son would accept the next suitable girl. In the previous village they were told of another settlement to the west, hit hard by raiders, and probably with little food left. Those people might be willing to let a girl go should they still have one—better that than have her stolen away by marauders...or die of starvation.

The boy interrupted the old man's silent musings, "It is time to go. It is still a long way to that village and the sun moves more quickly these days."

The boy's house had been finished for many weeks and needed only a woman to make it complete; one boy could not live in a house all by himself. His father's first thought had been they should go back to the old town to the south and try bartering for one of the girls his son had known as a child. But a passing traveler reported the town no longer friendly to those who had cast aspersions on its leaders... There would be consequences he said. Still that might have been a better way to go if the old man had known how hard this journey would be.

His father gauged the sun's place in the sky, nodded, and put the handful of piñon nuts in a small woven pouch at his belt, then took up his atlatl and long darts—nearly spears—that went with it. This was an ancient weapon but powerful and deadly in the right hands. Both travelers carried obsidian knives and a length of hand woven cordage, which weighed little and was good for all manner of things. Under his woven rabbit fur cloak the old man felt for the bag of turquoise beads and effigies. It was the wealth of their entire clan and in better times would have been more than enough to secure a wife. Now, such frivolous goods were not so valuable and in some places a bag of shelled corn or beans might bring more. No one had corn or beans to spare however. With winter coming on girls would not be needed in the fields, possibly even considered a drain on what little resources were left. This was not the way things of this sort were conducted in normal times, but things had not been normal for a very long time, and desperate people were now forced into desperate ways.

The boy's clan was poor, too, with few young people left. The elders grew determined in their efforts to bring in new blood before it was too late. Though he had only sixteen winters he was the oldest and most favored of the few young men left to the clan. It was true his sister's prophecies had something to do with his selection. She had long hinted to the elders that her brother would one day be a leader among them. He thought that might also be the reason he was chosen to have the new house. He was indeed the last best hope of the clan. He had not taken a war trail, but was already a good hunter and strong and fleet of foot.

When finally they reached the edge of the village the boy and his father stayed a good distance out but remained in plain view and waited for someone to come to them, that was the custom among their people. The dwellings sat on a promontory among the ravaged fields and the boy thought their houses pitiful and unprotected. He knew he and his father were being watched and evaluated by those behind the stone walls, but still no one came to greet them. Surely it was obvious what kind of people they were. They should be welcomed as friends, possibly even be mistaken for visiting relatives, as had been the case in the last community.

These later immigrants had chosen to occupy an earlier site from a time when there was little need for security. The boy thought them vulnerable there in the open and was glad his own elders had decided on a more protected place and then built with security foremost in their minds.

Finally, two older men cautiously appeared at the edge of a window and peeked out, still apprehensive and unsure. They were next seen covertly watching from a doorway; at last one moved into full view, held up a hand, and made the sign that acknowledged them as their own kind and welcome. Slowly, the pair moved out into the open and came closer. One man had something wrapped about his leg and was limping. Still somewhat leery, the two elders paused and took another careful look, then became satisfied these travelers were indeed of their own kind, and not enemies.

The boy's father, nearly as old as the other two, guessed them to be clan elders and soon convinced them of his mission—to find a suitable wife for his son. He said, "This boy will make one of your girls a fine and caring husband. He can hunt and is a good farmer... He will provide for her and defend her to the death."

The elders looked the boy up and down for what seemed a long space of time, then spoke quietly to one another; beckoned to them and led the way to their *kiva* and down the ladder.

After they had smoked their conical pipes and offered their guests cool water from an olla, one elder looked suddenly distraught, saying, "Until yesterday I had such a girl...my own daughter," he gritted his teeth. "She was snatched away with the others."

"No one followed to get her back?" The boy knew this was a rude thing to ask but time was short and he didn't look away as his father shot him a warning glance.

The older man had the scars of a warrior, and held up a hand to halt further talk from the boy. "I can see you are a plain talker but you are young, and not from around here, so I will let that pass." The man straightened and held his head higher. "We are not cowards. The first time a girl was taken we did follow and chased those people for a long distance. She was only a poor orphan girl too, but we thought it our duty to go after her and we did." The man's eyes grew bright with the thought of it. "Always it seemed her captors were just ahead of us. There were only two of them...but large men and swift. They had a noose around the girl's neck and forced her to keep up. We were five, all older as with myself, but still we thought once we caught up, we would make short work of them." Here the man paused, guilt plain upon his face. He hung his head and his voice sank to a whisper. "They were waiting for us beyond a small rise...along with three others. We fought them, but we are farmers and war is not our livelihood. Two of us were soon killed and two wounded, one seriously. There was nothing else for us to do but turn and run for our lives. Our worst wounded man made it back, only to die the next day." He choked and went silent and it fell to his companion to finish the tale.

"I was there in the front and first wounded," This taller man pointed to his calf, swollen and obviously painful. The black hole of an arrow wound oozed corruption despite the poultice around it. The man counted himself lucky, as it had only passed through the muscle. "We were able to break off the head and pull the shaft back out." He related this without emotion and continued in the same tone. "Though the girl was lost to us, we who escaped with our lives reconciled ourselves to that loss, thinking at least our people at home were safe. We had left our best fighters here to defend the village." Here neither man could speak and the boy and his father became uncomfortable, guessing what was to come.

The first man again took up the story, though his grief-stricken voice was still sometimes difficult to understand. "When we arrived here we saw several of the young men left behind to guard our families strewn about the ground as they had fallen. The raiders had been beaten back, two of them killed and two others so badly wounded they probably won't make it back north, but all at a terrible cost. Several women, wives of the dead men, were taken. Each had a child they fought to protect, but those were taken too." The man looked away and shook his head. "That may be just as well, their men are gone now and there is no one to provide for them. Even our dogs are dead, leaving none to warn us of another attack. Our hearts are broken." The man's shoulders slumped and shook, and though he continued to mumble on, no one could understand.

His companion touched the grieving man's shoulder and once again began to speak for him. "All of our young people are gone now and we old ones who are left do not have the will to hold this place." The old man leaned forward and addressed the boy. "So you see, when these last women were taken yesterday we knew it useless to seek revenge on the worthless dogs who took them. Now all we can do is keep ourselves barricaded within these stone walls. The raiders took everything in our storage bins and probably think they have everything worth taking now. They most likely will leave us alone for the time being. Probably they will be making their way north with their plunder."

"You will starve here this winter," The boy said simply and without thinking, but no one took exception this time. What was true was true and saying otherwise would serve no purpose.

The boy looked at his father and then at the two elders. "What is the clan of the girl that was taken?"

The girl's father looked up and scowled. "What does that matter now?" But there had been the fleeting hint of something in the boy's eyes and the old man was taken aback.

"What is the clan?" the boy asked again, but this time more gently.

Looking directly at him the girl's father whispered the clan name, peering hard at the boy through a veil of smoke.

The boy's father listened too, but had not heard of that clan in a long time, and it took a moment to remember who they were. He was afraid now of what his son might be intending...

The boy glanced at his father and saw him lower his head and then nod to the other old man. The boy persisted, "I do not know that clan, what does it mean?"

The old man raised his head and there were tears in his eyes. "It is their name for an ancient clan of the people. I thought them all gone now...the clan of the Swallow Keepers. The girl is the last of the Swallow Keepers."

The boy said no more, only gathered his few belongings and prepared to leave, motioning for his father to follow.

"Wait," The taller of the two elders stood and moved toward them. "If you intend to go after that girl we can help you with food...and there is an older boy left here, he can go with you. Some think he is not right in the head, but he is big and strong beyond his years...and he can fight."

The second elder, the girl's father, rose and came face to face with the boy. "I can see you have it in your head to find my daughter. I do not know you, but I can see now there might be more to you than I first thought." He put out a hand to touch the boy's shoulder. "Let your father stay with us and take the young man my friend has spoken of. It is his son and the one who killed two of those thieving dogs that cause us this heartache." He glanced sideways at his guest saying, "Your father is old and tired like us and will only slow you down. Leave him here. We have a buried cache of corn and dried squash and beans hidden not far from here. This is a good place to grow crops and is the reason we came so far from our old country. I see now that was a mistake and we have paid the price."

The old man looked from one to the other of his guests and then went on, "Our women have just this morning prepared food for our own journey. You can take what you need. Those marauders will think we are done and will not expect anyone from here to follow after them. They are heavily laden, and burdened with women and children. If the worthless dogs have not killed them already there will be two young women, each with a child, and the girl we spoke of. If you are spotted they will kill the children first." The old man's breath caught in his throat, "You can not save them all...or maybe none...and then it would all be for nothing. You are warriors now, you and that other boy, not farmers, and should it come down to it you must sell yourselves dearly, for there is greatness in that too."

The boy hesitated, looked to his father and saw the anguish in his eyes and knew the man had spoken the truth. "Wait here two days," he told his father, "And if I am not back, go south with these people. If I live I will find you."

The father gazed at his son as one already fading from his sight, "I doubt we will see each other again, but I will tell your sister you are now a man. Whether you live or whether you die, you will make us proud, just as she has always predicted you would."

5

The Fallen

Charlie Yazzie kept one eye on the clock as he shuf-
fled through the folder prepared for Police Captain
John Beyale. He hoped it would be enough to sway
the captain's decision in the matter of Billy Red
Clay's impending suspension. There were personal
references from prominent tribal leaders, and included several law enforcement officers Billy had worked
with. Charlie even hinted to FBI Agent Eldon Mayfield, that *he* might put in a good word. Billy had,
after all been his choice for Liaison Officer. Eldon
declined, saying the homicide investigation would
fall to his agency and propriety would not allow it.
Charlie had already figured as much, but thought the
agent might yet offer some less obvious support for
the young officer.

What Charlie had so far should, to his mind, be
enough to stave off suspension. Chief among the
documents was the deposition concerning the confrontation between Karl Hoffman and Billy Red
Clay—that would be key. Archaeology Professor
George Custer's signature on that one should carry

considerable weight. Charlie was, however, nearly certain Billy would remain a "person of interest," no matter what. That designation carried a weight of its own, sometimes making it hard for investigators to move past it.

The informal inquiry was scheduled for ten o'clock and Billy Red Clay asked that Legal Services Investigator Charlie Yazzie be allowed to present in his behalf. In view of the preliminary nature of the hearing, the captain was amenable saying the entire purpose of the meeting was to decide if further inquiry was warranted. Charlie Yazzie had acquired a certain status on the reservation and had friends in both high and low places. No one at tribal Police had been able to figure him out, therefore most thought it better to figure him in.

On the way over to the Federal Building Charlie wondered what the FBI might have come up with in the way of forensics in the murder and if they would see fit to share any of it with Tribal.

The autopsy report on Danny Hat was due in this morning as well. But that death now seemed almost forgotten in the excitement of the shooting. A connection between the two cases seemed likely to his way of thinking, and it would be interesting to hear what the FBI made of it.

The meeting lasted nearly an hour, at the end of which it was decided the young police officer, Billy Red Clay, would *not* be suspended, pending a more formal investigation. That Charlie Yazzie's input was a deciding factor in the decision was clear to Billy, and on the way out of the building he thanked the tribal investigator, several times. Both men were somewhat surprised to see Thomas Begay's truck in the parking lot and with both he and Harley Ponyboy sitting on the tailgate in what appeared to be a heated discussion.

"Harley, no one was stopping you from going back up to that *kiva*. You're the one who wanted to wait till the owl left."

"Yeah, but you wouldn' go with me neither."

"It was not my deal Harley! You're the one who thought you had something up there. I didn't know the prof was going to shut things down for the weekend."

Charlie and Billy interrupted the pair, Charlie asking, "What are you two doing in town? I thought you were on a tight schedule because of the road crew."

Thomas turned and grinned, shoving his chin at the load of groceries and water barrels filling the back of the pickup. "The professor said to pick up this stuff before we came back out today. It took a little longer than we thought."

Harley piped up, "The road crew shut down for the weekend due ta the 'accident' and George thought we all needed a break anyway, so he gave us a day off. We'll be on our way back up there here shortly—we just wanted ta hear what was up with Billy." Harley turned to the policeman. "I see you still got your badge Billy. Good for you!"

Billy Red Clay nodded. "It went better than I thought...thanks to Charlie I guess."

Charlie waved this off, "I think it's going to be all right, at least for the present."

Thomas hopped down from the truck. "That's good to hear, Nephew. I'd hate to see the reservation left unprotected." He then turned back to Charlie. "The professor is in town, too, said he had to check his mail and tend to a few things…like laundry." He grinned again and motioned Harley off the tailgate. "We're running a little late, we should already be back up there." Thomas was already in the truck when he hesitated and slid back off the seat. "Oh, I almost forgot, the Professor said he would drop by your office before heading back up to the dig. He said there was something he'd meant to tell you up there."

Back at his office, Charlie ran through his messages and saw there had been a call from Captain Beyale. When he rang him back the captain sounded in a hurry. "Charlie, we've had a further development in the Hoffman case." There was the sound of the officer clearing his throat. "Karl Hoffman's second in command has come up missing… I guess it could be anything…or nothing, but we are checking it out now rather than waiting. His name is James Erdric; his truck was discovered abandoned in a grove of trees just south of the road construction site. He has a trailer up there but it's locked…the caretaker says it's locked from the inside." There was a pause and Charlie could hear voices in the background. "I just thought I'd give you a heads up. I sent Officer Sosi up there to look into it and thought you might be interested in having a look around for yourself. I'm going to hold off on notifying the FBI until we know what we have here.

Charlie had no more than hung up the phone when he saw George Custer approaching the open door—apparently the receptionist had gone to lunch when he was on the phone with tribal.

The professor was smiling, but not for long, as he listened to the update on the latest happenings up at the construction site he said, "I'm on my way back up, I'll follow you if you don't mind?" Dr. Custer said nothing more as he fell in behind the tribal investigator.

~~~~~~

Thomas Begay and Harley Ponyboy finished unloading the supplies, and Thomas hand-carried the bags of more fragile items up to the professor's tent while Harley put the packsaddle on Jake and loaded the panniers with the more durable goods. The mule packed, but still had a little problem avoiding juniper trees along the path. After two days in the little three panel corral attached to the horse trailer Jake had finished the rather generous portion of hay Harley left him, and was nearly out of water—his energy level was way up and he showed this by banging his way through the trees. In the tent, Thomas could hear Harley cursing; the little man had come to believe it helped a mule pay attention, though he was yet to see much lasting good come of it.

Thomas went to the tent flaps and looked out. The lop-eared creature in question stood tied to a sapling. The packs had been offloaded and were sitting on a flat slab of rock. Although Harley was nowhere in sight Thomas could hear him quite plainly in the distance; still cursing. Harley wasn't ordinarily given to such language except when scolding Jake. When he found his friend on his hands and knees in the *kiva*, Harley had grown quiet. The little man had used up the list of curse words he was familiar with and was about to start over from the beginning, when he felt Thomas's hand on his shoulder and looked up.

"I can understand you cussing that mule, Harley, but I don't think it's gonna work on these rocks."

Harley shook his head. "...You said this thing had been here a thousand years and wasn't going anywhere...now it's gone."

"What's gone Harley?"

"Well, I don't know exactly... but someone's been into this vault and there's something missing," he said, gently blowing away the crumbling remains of what appeared to be some fibrous material leaving only the impression of something that had been half buried.

"You mean someone's been up here digging while we were in town?"

Harley snorted, "That's just exactly what I mean...looks to me like it was that first night, too." He reached to one side and picked up a small, shallow grey bowl the rim of which was decorated with tiny black swallows. "I found this over by the wall, wrapped in a rag. They must have lost it climbing out of the *kiva*. He held it up for Thomas to look at but didn't hand it over. There was a tiny hole drilled in the bottom. "You see that hole, this is a "killed" bowl and it was upside down over whatever was hidden under there. The slab was pried off, the bowl set aside and something taken. They must have been in a hurry not ta keep digging... that, or what they found was too important to risk staying any longer." The little man stood up and squinted down toward the road. "Whoever they were, they knew what they were doing." He paused and smiled. "Except for one thing."

"What's that Harley?"

"They brushed out most of their tracks… but they forgot this one under the rock cover they set aside. All's we got ta do is find who's wearing these boots."

Harley pointed at the only track still evident in the *kiva*. "The path up here is so rocky they didn't leave much sign except right here in the soft dirt where we've been digging."

Thomas stared at the track. "How do you know there was something under that bowl?"

Harley opened his hand. "These," he said. "These turquoise beads were scattered in the dirt around a hollow…an effigy or some sort of ornament or something. I can't make out what it was, but it had ta be something pretty special, probably strung on a necklace of beads." Harley gazed thoughtfully out past the *kiva*. "I'm pretty sure they waited for us to leave… then sneaked in here after dark."

Thomas peered up at the ceiling of the alcove rubbed his chin with two fingers and thought aloud. "I wonder how good they are at making owl hoots?"

Harley grimaced, "I already thought of that, I guess they know something about Navajos, too." Harley put the beads back where he found them, then carefully put the grey bowl back just as the ring in the dirt showed it had been and then replaced the stone slab. "The professor will want to take a look at this *in situ*," he said, proud of his latest archaeological term. He scratched his head. "I can't figure out why they didn't come back for that bowl the second night we were gone. It has to be worth five hundred, at least, on the black market"

~~~~~~~~

When Charlie and the professor pulled up at the construction site, Officer Hastiin Sosi was already there, speaking with the maintenance man, the same man Billy Red Clay had talked to the day of the Hoffman shooting. He was Indian, but probably not Navajo; he appeared worried, and seemed careful about how he answered the policeman.

Charlie stood back, not wanting to interfere with the *Tó'á háni* clan lawman; most Near to Water people he had known were a little high-strung at times and this one looked like he might be one of them.

Professor Custer nudged him and gestured toward a trailer whose door hung ajar. It had obviously been recently jimmied open, a crowbar still leaned against the siding, a number of flies were buzzing in and out and appeared quite excited about what was inside. Charlie nodded and the two moved toward the trailer—a shout from behind stopped them in their tracks, causing them to turn as the policeman waved them away from the trailer then held up a finger for them to wait. Hastiin Sosi wagged that same finger at the man he had been talking to, and pointed at a thirty-gallon drum. The man took this to mean he was to have a seat and wait, and this proved to be the case.

As the policeman approached, Charlie couldn't help but notice his right hand hovering over his sidearm, *this must be something new they're teaching at the academy*, he thought to himself. He remembered the professor mentioning the same thing in his deposition regarding Billy Red Clay on the day of the confrontation with Karl Hoffman. Over the past year or so Charlie himself had attended several state-mandated classes at the academy, but didn't remember this degree of readiness being encouraged.

At closer range, Officer Sosi saw the badge on Charlie's belt and then recognized the tribal investigator. Just the hint of a smile appeared at the corners of his mouth and his gun hand quickly reached to scratch his ear. "Sorry about that, Yazzie, but there's a dead man inside and all the usual people are on their way—like a herd of turtles—including the FBI, and you know how they are. As soon as I got the door open and saw what was what I just closed it back up. That's the way the FBI wants it."

Charlie gave him a conspiratorial wink followed by a halfway salute. "Not a problem, Hastiin." Then looking at the man sitting on the little oil drum he smiled, "You seem to have things well in hand out here and it's not our intention to interfere. It's just that your Captain Beyale suggested I come out and have a look, as he put it. I don't mean to get in the way, but there are a few questions a quick look inside might resolve."

The mention of his captain's name caused an immediate change in the policeman's attitude and he stuck out his hand. Charlie shook hands and introduced Professor George Armstrong Custer. Hastiin Sosi looked askance upon hearing the name but shook hands, all the while studying Charlie and the professor's face for some sign of a joke. When neither of the two men smiled or gave any indication this was not the professor's real name, the lawman cleared his throat and nodded vigorously, "Yes... well I'm sure it won't hurt for you fellows to have a peek at the remains. I know you won't touch anything. ...I'm sort of responsible you know... until the FBI gets here I mean. That Ute over there is the maintenance man, he says he heard this Erdric fellow come in late at night but said that was often the case and he didn't pay it any mind until this morning. When he didn't show up at seven this morning like he usually does he thought he'd better investigate. He couldn't rouse the guy so thought he might be sick or something and pried open the door. That's when he called the authorities."

Charlie and the professor smiled agreeably at this information and turned once more to the trailer. One look at the body was enough to convince them they'd rather read about it in the autopsy report when it came out. There wasn't much blood but what there was appeared almost black in the shadows of the trailer house. The body was sprawled across the floor, feet almost at the door, and it was obvious the person was trying to escape from someone, when he made it inside and locked the door before collapsing. Due to the trailer's off-road axles, the threshold was just below waist high and the men stood at the side of tall metal steps to gaze inside at the body, nearly within reach. The injuries, one obviously from a bullet, seemed to them more than sufficient to kill a man. The professor bit at his bottom lip and said, "That's the guy that was down at our camp with Karl Hoffman the other day."

Charlie hadn't mentioned the name Captain Beyale had given him that morning. "Are you sure? What was his name George?"

The professor peered over his shoulder. "I have no idea. Hoffman skipped the social amenities."

Charlie nodded and pointed. "His name is James Erdric... I believe some of those injuries might be knife wounds and serious ones, too. What do you think?"

The professor had looked away but dutifully glanced back at the corpse. "Maybe... I'm not sure." He'd seen all he had the stomach for and turned away. The professor had seen plenty of dead people, but most of them had been a thousand years old, and while some were remarkably well preserved, there still had been that certain detachment of time and culture. The remains of a person he had seen alive only three days before was an entirely different matter. George moved a short distance away before taking a fresh breath of air, leaving Charlie peering into the trailer where he reached unnoticed into the shadows and past the edge of the doorway.

The two men didn't wait for the FBI's entourage from Farmington, and only waved at the tribal policeman as they left. Officer Hastiin stood with one foot on the oil drum, his former detainee standing respectfully to one side, as Sosi took notes on a pad balanced on one knee. He was a very thorough policeman and determined to get things exactly right. He knew his words would soon be scrutinized by his superiors and dissected in minute detail.

Later, as Charlie and the professor rejoined the crew at the dig, preparations for lunch were underway. Thomas had put himself in charge of the meal, and had chosen one of his favorite midday snacks. He distributed small cans of potted meat and passed around a box of soda crackers to accompany them. He smiled at Harley, knowing it was a favorite of his as well. It was, in fact, Harley, who had taken it upon himself to add a case of this delicacy to the grocery lading. He apologized for not having bought the better brand with the little red devil on the label, but declared this to be nearly as good. Being both cheap, and readily available, potted meat has long been a favorite on the reservation.

In the old days, when Harley was a boy up in the *Tsé Bii' Ndzisgaii* a Navajo might refer to any meal time as "Lunch." Rising at daylight his grandfather might exclaim, "Get up everybody it's time for lunch!" Or at the evening meal, regardless of what it was, his mother might be heard to say, "Okay you people, lunch is ready." The old people still liked the sound of it. Lunch is an easy word to say in English and everyone gets it.

Charlie had eaten plenty of this particular brand of potted meat in his childhood, but had never really read the label. Now out of curiosity he held his can up close and examined the ingredients which caused him to make a little noise in his throat, after which he passed the remainder of the can to Thomas, who had finished his, and was quick to smile his appreciation.

Around reluctant nibbles of his last cracker, Charlie related what they had seen up at the road-camp.

Thomas looked over at Harley but addressed his question to Charlie Yazzie. "You say, you saw the dead guy?"

Charlie was still choking down the last of the cracker and before he could answer, the professor answered for him. "We saw him, all right. It was the guy that was down here with Karl Hoffman last week. He had apparently run into someone with a little less patience than us."

Harley coughed at this, his mouth dry from the crackers, and then reached for his water bottle before going on. "You didn't happen ta see what kind a boots he was wearing did you Doc?"

The professor and Charlie seemed a little surprised at the question, but Thomas wasn't, he had been about to ask that same thing himself and stopped chewing momentarily to hear the answer.

"Yes, his boots were right in front of us." Charlie didn't even have to think about it before answering. "Looked like the typical oil field boots to me, the kind any construction worker out here might wear." He pulled up the image of those boots in his mind and examined it before continuing. "They did have a little different tread pattern than I've seen before and a yellow logo imprinted in the heel."

Harley smiled and nodded. "A pattern on the sole like little plus signs... and a size nine maybe?"

Charlie again looked surprised. "I guess so." He looked at the professor. "What do you say George?"

"That's about right, I guess." George Custer was now looking directly at Harley Ponyboy. "This wouldn't have anything to do with what you wanted me to see up at the *kiva*, would it...? You really think it has something to do with the murder of this Erdric fellow?"

Harley laughed, "I would pretty much bet on it Doc. I put a cover over the track we found up there. Maybe those FBIs can do a match… but I bet it is the same guy."

Charlie looked from one to the other and wondered what he had missed.

6

1075 A. D.

The Pursuit

The hulking form of the young man from the village was barely visible in the darkness. He ran at a relentless pace and it was clear he didn't mean to stop any time soon. That was all right with the younger boy, he was a good runner himself and had no trouble keeping up.

The village elders had spoken the truth when they described their young man as big and strong. He was larger than most men the boy had known but probably only a year or so older than himself. He had yet to speak a single a word, whether unable, or just that he preferred quiet for the work ahead remained unknown. Both boys were adept at signing and had no trouble understanding each other.

Each carried a light pack of provisions, parched corn mostly, and wore cloaks of woven rabbit fur and turkey down. They carried their weapons slung on their backs. The younger boy had never seen such a lance as the other carried, heavy and long with a leaf-shaped chert point. Most likely it was from one of the raiders he'd killed at the village. The elders said he had no weapons of his own, finally admitting he was no longer allowed them, but didn't say why. The younger boy's father gave him his atlatl after hearing the young man was expert in its use. The pair carried no water as the older boy was familiar with the way north and knew of several seeps and tiny springs. There was still enough water to drink in that country should one know where to find it.

The younger boy had seen no lack of acuity in the other's thinking and wondered what was meant when the elders intimated he was not right in the head. Whatever problem this huge person had, there had been no sign of it, yet.

The first graying of dawn appeared in the east and quickly became streaked with red and orange mare's tails. In normal times this might mean rain was on the way. Now, it would probably be only a cold front moving through, pushing wind and dirt ahead of it. The tracks of the raiding party were easy to find and easier to follow. The village elder was right; the raiders *didn't* bother to hurry and showed little concern that anyone might come after them.

The boys kept their eyes on the trail ahead, slowing to a walk only when chewing their ration of corn. Twice, in the light of a waning moon, they stopped to sip water at hidden seeps, water that was alkaline and bitter, but they had drunk worse and were happy to have it. It was obvious the raiding party had been there before them each time, their prints plain around the muddy edges of the seep. The older boy gauged how long it took the dripping water to refill the pool below. He signed they might be only hours behind and should stay well back and wait their chance.

This made sense to the younger boy and he wondered again why anyone might think there was anything wrong with this person. They at last agreed it would be good to lie down and at least rest a while, that they might be fresh when the time came to strike.

It was light enough now to make better sense of the tracks and they saw there were only four of the raiders left. The other tracks were those of the three women in woven sandals. There was no sign of the two children. The women were carrying heavy packs of plunder and probably unable to help the children keep up, the missing tracks a likely indicator of their fate. When the older boy came to this realization he fell into an even darker mood and did not sleep. He sat brooding and watching through slitted eyes. One of those boys had been his nephew and often in his care. During the attack he had heard the boy call for him, but at the time had been busy killing a man with his bare hands and unable to save his nephew from capture.

It was close to sunset when the boys cautiously worked their way to a point above the trail and studied the way ahead. They knew they were close and no longer bothered to follow the trail itself, but kept to higher ground, out of sight or sound of the trail below. They lay on their bellies and carefully edged to the brink of the overlook. The invaders would make camp somewhere in the darkening canyon below, a place where there would be water and shelter from the coming weather. Even the older boy had not been this far north and now depended on the abductors to point the way to water.

"There," the younger boy finally whispered, "Below that ledge... just at the bottom."

The other instantly nodded, staring long and hard at the camp, which was nearly indiscernible in the shadows. They must remember exactly how everything was, and memorize a way down that would take them close, but afford cover for at least the first hour of descent. It would be dark after that and cover less important, but still they would have to move slowly and avoid the slightest noise. The moon would be only a sliver this night, and that would be to their advantage. They quickly shed their packs and readied themselves for the assault. *These marauders would not be taking their women to a victory dance tomorrow.* One way or the other this was as far north as they would go.

From the moccasin tracks the older boy had judged one, possibly two, of the attackers had suffered serious injury. One limped from time to time, and the other had a foot turned nearly sideways, causing him to stagger over the rough ground; he must be an important man not to be left behind. This and the heavy-laden women had slowed them considerably, even without the children.

This boy might get lucky—this boy who sought a wife to become a man. He showed courage enough now, but what would he do in the coming fight? The larger boy knew exactly what *he* would do and, despite the odds, he meant to take a heavy toll on these northern dogs. There was a reason even his own people feared the large and brooding boy.

As they studied the camp, the older boy reached in his pouch and withdrew a square of buckskin tied with a thong. He nudged the other, and handed him the package without looking, then surprised him by speaking his first words. "If these dogs should kill me, this will identify you to that girl who you would have for a wife. Her father is my uncle and told me to give you this, but only if I thought you worthy and a proper person." He smiled. "It is hard to see it now but that old man was a great warrior himself in his time––before he took to farming. He taught me what he could of how to go about it." He then frowned. "He thinks he sees something in you. I hope he is right. That girl down there is my cousin and is the only one who ever treated me well. She is the last of her clan; she will make a good wife." He turned to the boy, and in a voice devoid of feeling said, "My uncle told me; *if* I could not save her, then I must kill her…better that, than leave her to these wild men."

The boy was not shocked at this, only by hearing it spoken. Unfolding the buckskin he marveled at the amulet on its string of matching beads. Azure turquoise from the far southwest, a spider web of gold running through a delicately carved cliff swallow, so finely cut and polished as to take the breath away. He knew at once it was the work of master artisans in the old town. He could only nod, and for a moment did not trust himself to speak. Finally he said, "I hoped you would introduce me to that girl yourself and perhaps put in a good word for me." The boy smiled as he said this, but he meant it all the same, and as he saw the other attempt a smile in return, he said, "We are of the same people, you and I…our people left the great town for the same reasons. No matter if the worst happens here, we will surely meet again in another time and place."

With that, the two rose in the last faint rays of light and as they adjusted their weapons and put their minds to what lay ahead, the younger boy turned and asked, "What is your name brother?"

"I have no name. It has been lost to me." The young man did not explain, or ask what the other was called, there would be time enough for that later…or it would not matter.

As the pair silently, and with excruciating care, crept their way to the lower reaches of the canyon their minds were as one and each knew intuitively how the other was thinking. Their common goal was clear; they must kill four dangerous men. And if the women were to be saved, they must kill those men quickly. These were not the sort of people to leave a woman behind…not alive…that was certain.

It was growing late; it had taken nearly the entire night, to work their way off the rim. Ragged black clouds scudded across a scrap of moon, repeatedly plunging the canyon into full darkness. The wind rose with blowing sand and alkali dust so thick as to sting the eyes and fill their noses. If the moon didn't reappear soon, there was nothing to do but wait until it did. There could be no real plan—when the time came they could only do what fate decreed and hope it to be enough. The older boy would make the first move, as he was the more experienced and these women were his own blood. He knew they would get only one chance and lives, certainly their own, hung in the balance. When the pair thought themselves as close to the camp as they dared they could barely make out the sleeping forms. They still were not close enough to see exactly how things were, which were the raiders, and which the captives.

There would be a sentry. He would most likely be the most capable of their fighters—he must be first to die. Such a sentry should not be hard to locate and the older boy split off to circle the camp and search him out. The other waited a few minutes then moved in a different direction, bow at the ready, he would look for another target.

The marauders had no fire, and made little noise of any sort. They had become worried as they approached the mountains. They no longer felt safe, though it was the border of their own country. They now took precautions they had not bothered with before. Though wounded, the leader feared nothing from the farmers they left behind, but grew apprehensive as they entered their own land. He considered it even more dangerous here than below in the canyon country. There might be other roving bands here— possibly their own people and even more desperate killers.

The tired raiders ate parched corn from the stolen stocks and drank from the muddy seep. The women, in fear of their lives, had known better than make a sound. Later when one was heard quietly sobbing, she was instantly dealt a blow that silenced her, but that sound was heard, the location noted, and it became the start of a plan.

Should the two strongest warriors, likely sentries, be located and eliminated first, it would leave only the two wounded men to be dealt with. Not that they would be easy. Their injuries would make them no less dangerous—the first hint of trouble would alert them, and they would fight like animals brought to bay. Probably they were sleeping among the captives now, but should their prospects appear hopeless in the coming fight they were certain to wreak havoc on the helpless women. They would be deadly to their last breath.

The moon's tiny crescent appeared low in the sky, shed its clouds, and brought a rising wind to blow among the treetops, enough noise to cover the rescuers' advance. Easing into the deep shadow of a rock outcrop the older boy finally spotted the outline of a sentry. His atlatl was at the ready, a long dart already in place, but at the last moment the wind gusted and gusted again, and he thought the heavier, more powerful spear might be best. Just as he decided this and moved to switch weapons he saw the sentry twitch and jerk as if he had been dozing and come suddenly awake. It appeared he was turning to look directly at him…and it was then he saw the arrow through his throat and watched as the man crumpled to the ground. Even in so little light, and with the wind to contend with, the boy from the south had made a remarkable shot. *He must be very skilled to judge the wind so well as that…or he was very, very lucky.* Either way, he thought he had perhaps worried about this boy for nothing.

As he eased up to the lifeless body, the older boy had for the first time an unobstructed view of the camp itself. He saw five forms, motionless, all apparently sleeping. The two larger, one on each outer edge and tight against their packs would be last to taste his revenge. These and the dead sentry made three of the enemy now accounted for. Somewhere near the camp, there had to be a fourth, still hidden. These wild men were on their guard, and the boy gave thanks for the wind and passing clouds.

After loosing the arrow, the younger boy waited to make sure the first sentry stayed down. Only then did he become aware of his hulking companion; he had not seen him in the cover of the trees. He knew now they should immediately, and at any cost move on the sleepers. He made his first kill to avenge their people; whatever the price, and wife or no wife, he would now, and forevermore, be considered a man.

If there had indeed been two sentries they would have had signals, the call of a night bird perhaps. And now, because of him, there would be no answering call. A second sentry would be the final line of defense, probably was hiding near his sleeping companions. Both boys were of the same mind and screened by a growth of chokecherries soon came side by side. Not looking at one another they moved silently on the sleeping camp. The hoot of an owl brought them dead in their tracks; none of their own people would use the hoot of an owl to signal…too much chance it would attract that evil and maybe bring trouble. The two boys looked at one another— they already knew death was in the offing. The larger of the pair grinned and pushed his chin toward the sleeping camp.

As the sliver of moon came clear of the clouds the older boy turned to the other and nodded imperceptibly. His eyes glittered in the half-light, features contorted beyond recognition. So consuming a rage seemed to fall over him that the younger boy was for a moment taken aback. The heavy club of the dead sentry dangled from a thong on his strong left wrist. He signed that the younger boy should cover him as he advanced. It was clear he meant to fly upon these killers and have his revenge at any cost. The younger boy knew there would be time for only one shot at the hidden sentinel when he sounded the alarm. The two wounded raiders would be upon them then, as well and it would become a matter of clubs and stone knives.

The advancing boy was within feet of the nearest form before realizing it was not a person at all. They had been tricked. A woman screamed, and a mind-splitting cry erupted behind them. The younger boy had just moved behind a sapling and the arrow meant for him lodged there, nearly splitting the slender tree. Quick as a snake, he had two arrows in the air and before the crippled war leader could send another… one of his had found its mark.

The boy heard a guttural snarl of rage from his companion as he was struck a glancing blow from a spear. Blood spurted from his side even as he turned to face yet another furious enemy. The black streaked face told him it was one of those he had encountered in the fight for his village. The warrior erupted from beneath the leaves to slash at him once again, slicing deep into his upper leg and bringing him to one knee. But still, the powerful boy swung the stone club with a crushing blow to the side of his assailant's face. At the far side of the camp yet another warrior rose from cover and plunged a knife into the helpless captive beside him. With a last mighty effort the bleeding boy flung his big spear with stunning force, catching the earth-covered killer full in the breast, knocking him backwards where he lay good as dead beside the woman he had just killed.

Silence left by a dying wind fell over the camp as the younger boy searched wildly for yet another target. Nothing moved. Seconds flashed by and the boy with the club…dropped it. Although weak, he fixed a dart to his atlatl as two people broke from cover and fled across the clearing. The largest of the pair pushed a smaller person before him. The twice-wounded boy was certain it was his cousin; he feared for just an instant, that he was too far-gone and might only wound the frenzied killer…or hit the girl, who then might be dead either way. He cocked his arm for the throw and with a scream released the long dart. An arrow from the younger boy sang past him at the same instant, both projectiles finding their mark but neither with killing effect.

The boy nocked yet another arrow to his bow as he watched the girl sidestep a flint bladed knife and then deal her wounded captor a vicious kick to the groin. The man rocked to one side and caught a second dart from the atlatl through one eye. At nearly the same time the boy's last arrow pierced his body and he sighed, and was done.

The older boy cried a name, and this was the girl's first indication the attackers were her own people and not just another band of roving killers. As she sank wearily to her knees she saw someone running toward her and drew back, not knowing it was her future husband. When the boy slowed his approach and held out the amulet she knew she was indeed in the hands of people who meant her no harm.

The boy led her back to her dying cousin and she knelt beside him, saw there was no hope, and knew she would be the last of his people he would ever see. This was the second time he had killed in the girl's defense, the first time it had been an important leader of their own band. The boy was even younger then, but when the rage flew over him he would not be denied. Some said he was not right in his mind, feared him for it, and his name was no longer spoken.

"They will sing songs about you now," the girl told him, "And I will tell my children how you fought here today." The girl shed no tears as she watched the fire fade from his eyes, but spoke softly saying, "Go now Cousin, and help our dead find that far place where life is easy and there is no need to kill...your nephew is calling you." And then as the boy closed his eyes she whispered, "Your father will at last be proud and once again our people will speak your name."

7

Revelation

The salvage crew hurried themselves off to the *kiva* to inspect this latest find of Harley Ponyboy's, the one he thought might have some connection to the murder of James Erdric; late of the state highway department and now a suspected looter and thief, though a dead one.

As Harley got down on one knee at the stone lidded bin, the others gathered close and there was an air of expectation and curiosity on each face. Professor Custer leaned over Harley's shoulder as the slab was pried loose and lifted aside. The flat stone was set atop the bucket protecting the footprint he'd discovered earlier; the one he was certain belonged to James Erdric.

Harley pointed to the delicate bowl with the hole drilled in the bottom, and the professor was immediately on his knees, carefully lifting the delicate vessel to exclaim over the finely traced swallows decorating the inside rim.

Thomas threw a sideways glance at the professor. "That bowl was '*killed*' as a burial offering, that's why the hole?"

The professor turned to answer and was surprised at the distraught look on Thomas's face. "Yes," he admitted, "The bowl was intended to serve a person's spirit in the next world. This is most likely a burial." Then turning to the others he noted, "It's not often we see one so neatly drilled, but I imagine it was the surest way to insure a bowl didn't shatter in the *killing* of it. That *can* happen when a hole is chipped into the bottom." Dr. Custer shrugged. "I suppose some thought it didn't matter—a ghost vessel is a ghost vessel and will serve the dead either way."

Thomas Begay peered suspiciously around the *kiva*. "Ghost vessel? But these people didn't have *chindi* huh? Not like those evil *chindi* of the *Diné*, right?"

Charlie gave a tired sigh but caught himself before saying something he might later regret. "Thomas, no one really knows what these people believed. But after a thousand years I'm pretty certain there's nothing left here that can hurt you."

Professor George Custer agreed and smiled. "No, Thomas, these people didn't have evil *chindi*. As you can see they kept their dead close to them and didn't fear their spirits. The Navajo didn't come into this country until after the Anasazi were long gone; they had no beef with your people. The Utes might have been a different story, but for the most part even they got along all right—until the big drought—then it became a matter of survival for both and the Ute's ancestors might have played a harsher role. Eventually only these and maybe a few other outlier groups were left to roam this country. Some of them may well have been the descendants of the Paleo-Indians of the final glacial periods. We now call them the "Clovis" or "Folsom" people from right here in New Mexico and for more than ten thousand years."

Quiet contemplation followed the professor's timeline, and the spell of those ancient people lay heavy about them.

All this time Charlie scarcely listened to the professor or looked at the bowl, instead just stood staring at the few turquoise beads scattered about, and the impression left by something he thought must indeed be very rare. He reached in his pocket and pulled out the three beads he had picked up at the murder scene and tossed them among the others.

Harley looked up, brightened, and guessed. "You pick them up at Erdric's trailer?"

Charlie nodded; everyone could see the beads were identical and from the same type turquoise.

The professor stared at his former student and was momentarily at a loss of what to say.

~~~~~~

The next day when details regarding the double homicide began coming in, Charlie perceived a decreasing interest in the death of Danny Hat. He was now apparently considered no more than a petty offender who ran out of luck. As it turned out the young Hopi was only wanted for questioning in a drug related incident, the report of which, was in itself questionable in Charlie's view. Why the FBI had issued a warrant for so trivial a matter wasn't clear. Charlie made note of that as well. The autopsy report *had,* apparently revealed a considerable level of amphetamines present in Danny Hat's system. He had a record of drug use and amphetamines seemed to be his drug of choice. Actual cause of death was deemed heart failure, brought on by dehydration and overexertion, exacerbated by the amphetamines. The cause of death was ruled "natural causes." There had been no indication of foul play. Now, three members of the same road crew were dead, and all within a like number of days, yet nothing connected Danny Hat to the two homicides. Charlie thought there might be more to his death than was indicated in the reports.

The tribal investigator was just finishing with the FBI portfolio, including the preliminary autopsy results in the two shootings, when his intercom buzzed and the receptionist announced he had visitors. He glanced through the glass of his office door and drew an exasperated breath. Thomas and Harley, like most of his people, never offered advance warning of a visit, just "dropped by" whenever the mood struck them—totally without regard for a person's plans or schedule. Charlie supposed this went back to a time when his people had no schedule and made few plans.

Thomas was grinning as he came through the door and turned to hurry Harley along. The little man had stopped to chat with the *Sash dine'é* woman at the desk. She was new, and Harley thought the Bear People Clan interesting, especially one as pretty as this. He was about to make known his own clan affiliations, which was the proper thing to do when two single people met, but was interrupted when Thomas put two fingers to his lips and gave a sharp whistle.

Harley smiled at the young woman, held up a finger and said, "I'll catch you later Louise. My friend and I have some business with Mr. Yazzie," thinking this sort of talk might impress her. He then turned, grinned, and said something unintelligible under his breath.

Several of the staff had taken note of the pair's noisy entrance and Charlie hurried to shut the door behind them, then frowned out at the girl, who blushed and turned back to the switchboard.

"She's a little young for you, isn't she, Harley?" Charlie was joking, of course, but Harley Ponyboy appeared to take him seriously, looked down, and again muttered something no one heard.

Thomas, already sprawled in a chair across from Charlie's desk, laughed, causing Harley to shake a finger in his direction.

"So what brings you two to the hallowed halls of justice this morning?" Charlie doubted it was anything of any great import, but had at times been surprised by the pair.

"Oh, nothing much," Thomas reached down and pulled off a boot to examine the toe of a sock, then tipped the boot up and shook it. "Feels like a little rock in there somewhere…" He said this as though it excused their intrusion and might serve to answer the investigator's question, all in one.

Charlie nodded and grinned over at Harley, who mistook this for an apology, smiled in return, then said, "The Doc told us we could meet him here this morning, he owes us money and we're gonna' try ta get some of it."

Thomas quickly interjected in the professor's behalf. "The Doc was just a little light this week, that's all. He's having to bid these jobs so low he's having trouble making the payroll...he's just a little light."

Charlie again nodded, but still wondered why they chose his office to settle their finances. He glanced at the clock. "When exactly was all this supposed to take place?" He said 'supposed to take place' in deference to the well-known Navajo predilection for bending time to fit convenience. Some of this same concept appeared to be rubbing off on Professor Custer who seemed to have adopted a like attitude of late. Charlie thought he might be hanging out with Thomas Begay and Harley Ponyboy too much.

Thomas himself shot a glance at the clock. "Oh, I expect he'll be along directly, he probably had to drop by the bank...it's almost lunch time." Thomas smacked his lips at the thought. "Maybe he'll take us all to lunch?"

"It's a little early for lunch." Charlie felt mid-morning a tad short of lunchtime; still, he wouldn't put it past Thomas to make it happen.

Harley pointed his chin at the tall stack of papers on the desk and said, "You writing a book?" chuckling at his own joke, apparently the only one who found it amusing.

"No, Harley, this happens to be the FBI's version of why they have three dead people on their hands and not a clue as to why."

Thomas thought this hilarious and gave Charlie a thumbs-up, then hooked the same thumb toward the door and raised his eyebrows at Harley. "The boss is here." He waved through the glass-paneled door and beckoned the professor back to Charlie's office.

Dr. George Custer had the look of a man resigned to his fate. He glanced from one to the other before throwing his hands in the air. "They've got us shut down boys, but thank God, they shut the road crew down too. The FBI wants the rest of today to finish their investigation out at the dig…and another 24 hours to evaluate what they've found…then maybe they'll decide if they missed anything and have reason to go back and re-evaluate any part of it."

The professor brightened and continued, "The road crew will have it even worse though. 48 hours for them, and the DOT may keep them down longer depending on how long it takes to bring in new crew. They say it's their heavy season and they're short-handed." The professor chuckled despite himself as he dragged up another chair. "It might be a week before they're up and running again. This just might give us the lead time we need to catch up out there." His two employees sat looking at one another for a moment and considered how this new development might further affect their lives.

Thomas finally shook loose the pebble in the toe of his boot, placed it back on his foot, and then wiggled his toe in happy affirmation. Glancing again at the clock he looked at the professor and mentioned the Diné Bikeyah would be serving lunch in thirty minutes.

Harley was more to the point. "Doc, you didn't happen to bring us a little money did you?"

George Custer reached in his pocket and said, "Boys I can let you have twenty apiece, cash, right now…and I'll buy lunch."

Harley smiled at this and was amenable.

Thomas, for his part, liked nothing better than a free lunch, and both men appeared well satisfied with what they would later refer to as their *negotiations*.

Charlie shook his head at the two and motioned them to the door. "Today's payday for everyone here in the office, too. We better go now if we want to beat the crowd."

The Diné Bikeyah Café was, as predicted, filling fast and the men were lucky to get a table in the back. The "special" board listed the usual selection. A Navajo taco or the cheeseburger deluxe—which included fries, unlike the base model, which didn't.

The professor glared at the menu board. "Just once I'd like to come in here and see something other than cheeseburgers or Navajo tacos on special."

Harley scoffed, "You should have come last week, Doc. It was chicken fried steak and all you could eat fries for $5.99." then added, "Thomas loaded up."

"I'm sure he did, Harley, but don't you guys ever get tired of the same old thing?"

Thomas eyed the professor. "George, this place would go out of business if they didn't offer cheeseburgers on the Special."

The professor sighed and ordered a BLT, knowing the bacon was never done to suit him and it came with only a slice of dill pickle on the side. "So, Charlie, what's the latest the FBI has to say about the shootings?"

"Well, Captain Beyale sent over a copy of the preliminary reports they gave him, but the actual lab reports won't be in for days yet. And we still don't know how much the FBI's actually letting out. As usual the Feds only give us what they want us to know. At least that's been the case in the past." Charlie had long been an advocate of more transparency among the agencies, but thought little progress was being made in that direction.

Thomas pointed toward the crowded entrance. "Here comes trouble," he said grinning.

It was tribal policemen Billy Red Clay and Officer Hastiin Sosi, who immediately spotted the group and began working their way to the back of the restaurant. The policemen shook hands all around and pulled up chairs. Billy's eye appeared to be healing; the bandage had been removed to expose a neat little row of stitches.

"You're looking better Nephew. How are you feeling?"

"I'm good Uncle." He then glanced over at Charlie. "Still no word on when my review might happen…but at least I'm not on suspension."

"Well, Billy, I suspect no news is good news in this case." Charlie wasn't sure this was true, but knew it was what the young officer wanted to hear.

Hastiin Sosi spoke up, addressing both the professor and Charlie who sat side by side. "When you gentlemen were up at the construction site you didn't happen to notice any turquoise beads, did you? By James Erdric's body, I mean? I could have sworn there were seven or eight scattered around when I got the door open but the FBI photos show only four as far as I can see."

Charlie spoke first, "I really couldn't say Hastiin; I guess I was more focused on the body itself."

Dr. Custer nodded. "I did notice a few beads but didn't stop to count them. Why do you ask?"

"Oh, no reason, I guess, they could have rolled under something when everyone was tromping in and out, but those boys are usually pretty careful when it comes to stuff like that." The tribal officer sounded casual, nearly offhand, but his eyes narrowed as he looked from one to the other. "I just coulda' sworn there were more of them."

Billy Red Clay interrupted and glanced over at Charlie, "I've been poking around a bit the last two days and have found a few things you might be interested in—though it could be just more reservation rumor."

Charlie perked up. "What's that Billy? Every little bit might help, you know."

Billy hesitated, glanced over at his fellow officer, and continued. "You probably know Danny Hat's mother is a full-blood Hopi and Danny's father was Hopi as well. Come to find out the mother is pretty well thought of back home...despite her later marrying a Navajo. Her first husband died in a car accident when they still lived on the Hopi reservation. Now it seems she has family who want her to move back and run for council."

"You mean Danny Hat was full-blood Hopi?" Charlie was somewhat surprised to hear this, though he wasn't exactly sure why.

Judging from the expression on his face this was also news to Harley Ponyboy. The little man, looking perplexed, admitted, "That would explain a lot about Danny, for one thing he was always more interested in Hopi stuff than Navajo...you know, religion and things like that. His sister Luanne wasn't that way at all, but she was younger and half *Diné*." He thought a moment. "Come to think of it Luanne really wasn't much on religion, of any kind."

Billy Red Clay looked at Harley. "Didn't you and her used to hang out together? I seem to remember you two being together a lot when I was a kid."

Harley squirmed in his chair. "No, not really, She was one of those girls who had a lot of boyfriends."

Thomas grinned. "You seen her lately, little man?"

Harley blushed. "We been out a time or two. She says she has a few problems to work out."

Hastiin Sosi grinned along with the rest and then grew serious. "Charlie, there is one other thing you ought to know. The man I was questioning the day you and the professor were up at the construction site was Jimmy John, a Ute who lives just across the state line, not far from the road construction site. He told me no one liked that supervisor, Karl Hoffman, or his friend James Erdric either. Neither of the two liked working with Indians, kept mostly to themselves, and didn't mix much with the crew after work. He said Erdric was supposed to be some sort of an engineer or surveyor or something. Jimmy seemed to think Erdric had some sort of hold over Hoffman."

Charlie frowned, "Did he say what sort of hold?"

"No, but he thought whatever it was gave Erdric plenty of say in what went on, almost like he was the boss instead of Hoffman.

Dr. Custer looked across the table at the tribal policeman and persisted. "He didn't know why that would be?"

"He said he didn't, but mentioned bits and pieces of a conversation between them and a man named William Crawley who came by on several occasions. This 'Crawley' person also seemed to defer to Erdric."

Charlie and Professor Custer exchanged looks and the professor cleared his throat before asking if the Ute maintenance man had mentioned anything about suspicious activities around any of the smaller ruins in the area.

"I don't think that ever came up, Professor." Hastiin pulled a small notebook from a breast pocket and said, "I have directions to Jimmy John's home-place written down if you would like to talk with him yourself. He's lived around there all his life—his family runs cows all over that country." The officer jotted down instructions on how to find Jimmy John's camp and passed them to Charlie who looked them over, nodded, and passed them along to the professor.

Putting the directions in a shirt pocket, the professor thanked both officers saying if there was ever anything he could do for either of them they shouldn't hesitate to ask.

~~~~~~~~

Charlie Yazzie and George Custer said very little on the way back to Legal Services.

Finally, Charlie asked him straight out, "George, we've known each other a long time...I'm getting the impression something's bothering you...I mean beyond the dig and keeping ahead of the road crew."

Custer remained silent, watching out the side window as they passed through the dusty, windblown streets of Shiprock. He finally turned to Charlie but reflected on the question another moment before answering, "I guess being constantly outbid on these projects lately could have something to do with it. When the other outfit first started picking up the contracts I thought it was my fault for not watching expenses...or possibly taking too much time with the sites. But after a little soul searching, I realized the work couldn't be done any quicker, or cheaper...not and provide any reasonable amount of documentation of both the site and the specimens recovered."

The professor paused, pointed out his truck at the far side of the parking lot, and went on. "Most sites here in the Four Corners have been worked over for the past hundred years or so. Pot hunters mostly—it's almost a tradition among the locals in some places." They pulled alongside George's old Suburban and Dr. Custer went on. "Despite increasing federal legislation it's still happening today. Of course, many of our original champions of southwestern archaeology were little better than glorified pothunters themselves. I could name more than a few." The professor stopped, and looked around the parking area before shaking his head and continuing, "Massive undocumented collections were shipped to universities back east, even to several European collectors and museums. A few of those early collections are still considered the crème de la crème of Anasazi culture, especially those from Mesa Verde and eastern Utah." The professor grew irritated and exclaimed, "Why, a museum in Finland is said to have one of the finest collections of Mesa Verde specimens in existence...some consider it better than the onsite museum at the mesa itself. Those exhibits, even today, rely on artifacts on loan from local families and educational institutions. Losing their burial displays due to the Reparations Act left a big hole in their collection."

The professor looked tired as he reached for the door handle but was not finished. "In the thirties, museum and university sponsored expeditions into this country heated up, and the Anasazi craze was on." Custer chuckled in spite of himself. "There were nationwide newspaper accounts of the latest finds and those fueled a race to fill exhibition cases. They made media darlings of certain previously unknown archaeologists and even some avid amateurs—who in most instances were doing little more than salvage work themselves." The professor fixed Charlie with a grim smile. "In any case, new and important finds *are* still turning up, and it's the duty of people in my business to see they wind up in the right hands." The professor opened the door slightly, but still sat quietly in his seat as though in thought. "Even the term 'Salvage Archaeology' has taken on a different tone, which is why most in my line of work now refer to it as 'Contract Archaeology'. Just a matter of semantics I suppose, but there you have it."

As the professor got out of the truck he hesitated again and shrugged. "There is one other thing Charlie, you'll recall Officer Sosi mentioned the name William Crawley. Years ago a William Crawley was with UNM, until he was inexplicably discharged, and under undisclosed circumstances. In the old days the university was more careful of their reputation and seldom made public the reasons for letting someone go. I later heard he had worked for a while on a dig in Guatemala, but again, was dismissed. I lost track of him over time, today was the first time I've heard his name in years. Assuming it's the same man, of course. I just find it curious, that's all."

After the professor pulled out, Charlie sat a few minutes thinking about what had been said. He knew several early cultures had evolved on what is now the Navajo reservation. There were, in fact, several national monuments devoted to them, and they drew thousands of visitors a year. They had, over the years, become an important financial resource for the tribe. But it was big country, and there were still those few *Diné* who were not afraid of the ancient ones and were sometimes even willing to come up with the occasional artifact, if the price was right. Charlie thought his own people should be taking more responsibility for these ancient sites. Protection of "Cultural Heritage Sites" was not only in the interest of the general public, but that of the Navajo people as well.

8

1075 A.D.

The Way Back

The boy and girl spent the rest of that horrific day of the battle, burying the dead, but only by heaping on rocks to protect them from animals. The marauders were left as they fell. The recovered packs of grain and other plunder were concealed in a hidden fissure, rocked up and secured behind a curtain of brush. The boy thought it would do until they could bring help to retrieve them.

Though it was nearly dark by the time they finished they were determined not to stay another night in that place, and began their weary climb out of the canyon. When they reached the high ledge where he and her cousin had left their packs, he deemed it far enough. Still they did not make a fire or eat other than parched corn from the packs.

They were still three days hard travel from the boy's village, and though heavily laden, they were young and strong and spurred on by hope of what might lie ahead for them. The girl knew of several short cuts and he was now thinking they would make better time than he and his old father, when *they* had last come into this country. Those people left in the girl's village would have already headed south and he hoped his father was with them.

They spent a cold and restless night and the girl shivered despite the woven feather and rabbit-fur robe from her dead cousin's pack. As the sun rose they were well on their way, and both had time to think as they jogged along under their heavy loads. The boy was certain the girl's people were not far in advance and knew they would be taken in by his clan. His father would see to that. *Were he and the girl not to be married? They would all be family then. And her people brought their own store of food...that would be in their favor, and too, there were still their stolen caches hidden safely away to the north. The newcomers would be people of substance and he was certain they would be treated as such.*

The girl kept her thoughts to herself and tried to convince herself of the debt owed this boy who had come for her, despite the many dangers. She had to admit he had many of those qualities generally looked for in a husband, a little young perhaps, but still older than she, and with the skills and intelligence to one day take his place at the council fires. He was not as big or as fierce as her cousin, but had given a good account of himself and she doubted the rescue would have happened without him. He was of the people from the old town to the south and of the old blood—unlike her cousin, whose mother had been chosen by the Holy Ones, then later discarded.

When the woman came back to her people, it was because she had no choice, then she had the son that would forever be an outsider; shunned and whispered about behind his back. Always, the boy had a hidden rage lurking just below the surface. Some thought he went too far to the outsider's blood, through no fault of his own. She knew her father would have had him banished...if he were not his sister's son.

Her young rescuer carried his bow in his left hand, and three of the arrows plucked from his enemies were back in their quiver, the heads now set in enemy blood. The girl carried his father's atlatl and the few long darts that were left. The women of his clan were well versed in the use of weapons and he assumed this girl would know at least something about them. At the last moment, the girl picked up the stone-headed club her cousin had dropped; although it was heavy she was determined to have it as a remembrance of him and his part in the death of her captors.

Once they topped out of the canyon the way would grow somewhat easier and while they would pass through the girl's home village, the boy had decided to avoid the next two settlements after that, those he and his father had passed through on their way up. Their heavy packs might arouse people's curiosity and perhaps even cause them to be jealous. Nothing was as it once had been, nor would it ever be again. What lay ahead was uncharted and each day could only be taken as it came.

~~~~~~

The boy left everything, including the girl, hidden in a cluster of cedars then cautiously circled her old village, watching for some time before deciding it safe…only then did he go back for her.

The village was abandoned, leaving only an old woman who lie dying at the side of the elder with the wounded leg, already dead of infection. He had sent his woman's only child to extract revenge, a boy he considered his son, but he would never know the outcome. The old couple was left food and water but there was little else to be done. It was the survival of the many that was paramount now; the old people knew that and could only wish their relatives luck on their journey.

The two young people spent the night in the girl's family quarters. She unearthed a hidden cache of sandals and her sewing pouch to add to her pack, along with a shallow bowl, which she carefully wrapped in a piece of buckskin. Her mother had made her that bowl. She had helped decorate it with tiny swallows around the inside rim.

The boy judged they were only a day behind her people now and thought they might easily catch them the next day. There were still those who could not travel so quickly, and that included his father. The girl made a careful tally and judged there should be no more than ten or twelve of her people left, and they mostly women, two or three with children. Her mother and father should be among them as far as she could tell. They had taken everything they could carry, and she was glad they would not go as beggars in these dark times.

The next morning when the girl went to check on the old woman, she was dead. Since the remains were protected in an inside room, they were only covered with woven mats and left as they were. Time was short and neither could say what awaited them down the trail.

The pair gave a wide berth to the other villages in their path and, by the sign the girl's people left, knew they had done the same. They encountered no trace of raiders and were now far enough south they thought themselves safe. The boy concentrated on catching up to the girl's relatives, possibly only a short distance ahead. If that were the case, they would find them not far from his village and able to make a proper entrance without causing undue alarm. The boy would be returning as a man, with a wife and a new home waiting, not to mention additional people to share the work of building and bring fresh blood to strengthen the clan.

He would have to speak with his sister and see what guidance she might offer to secure their future. Who could say what she already had planned... certainly more than he.

~~~~~

Autumn lingered, as the boy and girl readied their new house for winter, and the girl's people settled in and allied themselves with the others. It was then the elders decided it was time a party should return north and retrieve the hidden stores before the first blizzards tore through the canyon and brought life to a standstill. Then there would be time to gather in the *kiva* and warm themselves at a common fire while they told stories and sang the old songs to their ancient Gods. *This is what separates us from those others in the town to the south,* the boy thought—those people he once tried not to think of, and now seemed to have trouble remembering.

Frost laced the ground the morning the little band gathered to go north. The boy and girl would show the way and would again avoid the settlements––hoping they would neither hear nor see those people—if indeed any were left in that wild land. No one could be trusted now.

The way north was uneventful. The caches were found just as they had been hidden. The stories of the battle were again told and the account of the girl's cousin and his fearless attack became an even greater source of pride and strength for those of her people.

The animal-ravaged remains of their enemies were mute evidence of the fierce encounter and most thought it a miracle that even one girl captive had been saved. The graves of their people were properly mourned; their fate became a further incentive to be on guard and away from that dangerous country as quickly as possible.

Just before dark, on the second night of their homeward journey, the boy's wife spotted a single small girl near the mouth of a rocky draw and would have pursued her if the men had not called her back. It couldn't be certain the child was alone they said. Silently, several men dropped their packs, and keeping only their weapons gave chase, thinking the child might be of their own people. They were aware she might be a decoy but thought, *Surely raiders would not have bothered with so small a girl.*

The child first hid from them. She had not eaten in a while and was weak and fearful. When they drew near she ran, but soon stopped and turned when she heard her pursuers call to her in her own language. The men brought her back and allowed the women to decide what should be done with her. It would be foolish to leave her out there where she might give them away or tell others what she had seen.

They found no sign of others and eventually learned the girl was from the second of the two villages that lay beyond their own. That night after camp was made, and with only a little coaxing from the women, the child related her story of hiding in the underbrush as her people were attacked and the village destroyed. The girl was sure she was the only one left, and it was decided to take her along rather than leave her to an almost certain fate. Perhaps the Gods had brought them this girl and who could say what plans they might have for her.

~~~~~~~

Winter settled in late, but with a vengeance, blizzard after blizzard howled through the canyons, leaving deep snow to hinder travel and make difficult the collection of firewood or hunting. By the month of popping trees, even the oldest could not remember it being so cold.

And it was then the wolves of winter began to appear—first only one or two, who watched silently from the other side of the canyon; finally, shrugging deep into their blankets they went away. This village on the cliff was not like those to the north; this one would not be so easy.

9

The Informant

FBI Agent Eldon Mayfield took it upon himself to personally notify the professor his work could resume. He surprised George when he appeared interested in the little ruin and seemed curious to hear more about it. "I've read some," he admitted, "After being transferred to the area, and while such things don't fall under our agency's specific jurisdiction, they still *are* under federal mandate." The agent paused, and then, as though he had memorized it from a text said: "All federal agencies should at least understand the problems facing the preservation of these historic sites."

The professor was delighted to hear this and immediately launched into a rather detailed overview. "This little site most likely escaped serious attention due to the overgrowth obscuring the alcove. It's been dug in over the years, of course, all of them have, but it's never been extensively excavated. Other than a few shallow potholes the *kiva* remains almost untouched." He emphasized several unusual features of the little complex and how they differed from others in the area, then went on to mention several of the other ruins recently worked over by looters.

The FBI man shook his head and frowned over this. "I'm sure the Department of Interior would be interested in those reports." The Federal agent hesitated, and then continued almost reluctantly. "I've recently been made aware of rumors… Professionals, collecting and selling artifacts on the sly." The FBI agent said this in an unassuming manner, seemingly not calculated to include the good doctor.

The professor nodded thoughtfully and appeared not to consider the information accusatory, though secretly, he was beginning to think the FBI man's visit might have been more than just a courtesy call from the beginning.

Harley Ponyboy and Thomas Begay, who had remained slightly out of hearing till now, sensed things were not going well and thought the offer of lunch might be a good idea. Ever cautious in the presence of the law, the pair edged forward and wondered aloud to the professor if he wanted them to start lunch, and for how many.

Taking this as a hint the FBI man excused himself, despite the professor's insistence he stay on for the noon meal. "No," he said, "I'd best be getting back to Farmington. I have a meeting this afternoon, and what with the road being torn up it makes for a long drive." He turned privately to the professor. "The agency will be finishing up its reports in the next day or so. I'll let you know should I need anything further regarding your people's altercation with the two murdered men."

The professor smiled and again nodded, but thought this last sounded somehow ominous. As he stood watching Eldon Mayfield gun the government car up onto the roadway, it occurred to him that there might be more to his statement than he let on. He understood now why Charlie Yazzie displayed a certain reticence when dealing with the man. He would have to be more careful what he told the agent in the future.

~~~~~~~

Paul T'Sosi stood, hat in hand, waiting for the receptionist to buzz Charlie Yazzie's desk phone. He had no idea what he would say to the tribal investigator, but thought it important he at least let him know what he'd heard. It would never have entered his mind to go to any regular law enforcement officer with it. Paul T'Sosi was not in the habit of divulging the secrets of those who sought his services. When the buzzer sounded, the old man could hear it even at the front desk and wondered why the woman hadn't just called out, instead of going through this electronic rigmarole. *Why did these people have to make everything complicated?*

Charlie leaned slightly to one side for a view of the outer office and seeing the old man, waved him back, then smiled as Paul set the new black Stetson on his head and made his way through several occupied desks to the investigator's office. The old man wore the hat in the old fashion; flat brimmed, with no crease. Several office workers smiled as he passed but he paid them no mind, looking neither to the right nor left.

"Come on in Paul... I see you have a new hat." Charlie gave the hat an approving nod.

"Yes, my daughter thought the old one a disgrace and bought this new one for me. Her blankets are selling well and these days she spends money like it's water, new house, inside bathroom, a telephone, and is talking about a new truck." He smiled, "There was nothing wrong with that old hat; I'm sure it would have lasted at least as long as I will."

The two men grinned, knowing he was probably right. "What can I do for you today, Paul? Nothing in the way of legal problems, I hope."

"No, it's more in the line of what I can do for you that I have come."

"Ahh... and that would be?" Charlie was used to a long and convoluted prelude to any conversation with the older *Diné*, and was surprised when Paul came directly to the point.

"Yesterday, Danny Hat's sister came by our place. She talked about Danny for a while saying their mother had taken his death pretty hard and all. But when she got down to business she said Harley Ponyboy told her I might be able to help with a little problem she's having."

"Oh? Nothing too serious, I hope."

"Yes, I am afraid it is serious. She admitted she and Danny have been using drugs for a while now— after his death she decided she might better quit while her mother still had a child left." Here the old man lifted an eyebrow. "Harley Ponyboy told her I might be able to help her with that. She told him she didn't want to go to Health Services. She was afraid some of those girls down there would talk it all over the reservation—she didn't want her mother to know."

"Have you talked to Harley about this?

The old man gave a vigorous shake of his head, which caused his hat to go awry. Frowning, he reached for a tissue from the box on the desk, folded it lengthwise several times and tucked it inside the hatband. After squinting an eye at the job, he placed it firmly back on his head and appeared satisfied with the fit. "I told Luanne, curing that sort of thing was best left to white medicine, and probably I could not do much about it, at least not 'til she was clean... then maybe we could work on getting her *hozo* right."

Charlie frowned and fixed the old singer with a wry smile. "I knew from the autopsy report that Danny's death was probably drug related, but it's interesting Harley knew about Luanne and never said anything about it. We were talking about her only a few days ago."

Paul T'Sosi shrugged. "You know Harley, he don't like to point no fingers. He's been know'n Luanne since they were kids and probably thought I could help make this thing go away and no one the wiser." He pulled the Stetson back off his head with a frown and inspected the packing, adjusted it slightly, then paused and brushed a bit of dust from the brim. "The thing I really came about...I know now where Danny Hat was getting the stuff. She didn't mean to tell me but she was upset and it just slipped out."

Charlie brought his chair upright and leaned forward.

The old man narrowed a cautious eye toward the door. "I would not usually say anything about something told me in confidence, but in this case I don't see how I can stay quiet about it. There's been two murders already and another person's death as well, and who knows if it will end there." Paul lowered his voice to the point Charlie had to lean even closer to hear. "It was that man from the road crew…James Erdric."

Charlie hadn't realized he was holding his breath, and let it out with a sigh, as he motioned Paul to continue.

"Danny Hat was paying for the drugs with artifacts, pottery mostly, from the ruins the road crew was plowing up. That's why only he and Karl Hoffman operated the bulldozer. Luanne said they stayed in advance of the crew and Hoffman was good at what he was doing, knew how to skim off the top layers, and leave the good stuff more accessible." Paul grimaced, "I'm sure they ruined a lot, but they did most of their work on weekends, after the crew went home, and were probably able to salvage a good bit." The old man settled his hat back on his head, giving the brim a good tug this time to fix it in place. "I think Luanne might be wrong about her mother not knowing what Danny and her were doing. Martha Keyoni is no fool and she has ears everywhere." The singer then stood, indicating he was through talking and had said what he came to say.

After Paul T'Sosi left, Charlie sat trying to put it all together in his mind. He was now convinced there was a link between Danny's death and the two murders. He thought he would have to pay Luanne a call and he would take Harley Ponyboy along too, just so everyone would be on the same page. He would have to talk to Police Captain John Beyale about the Ute Jimmy John.

~~~~~~

Sue Yazzie had spent nearly an hour talking to Lucy Tallwoman before she realized Charlie would be home soon and there was still dinner to make. Now that she and Lucy both had phones they thought it silly not to use them. Not many other people they knew had phones, so for the most part they talked only to each other. Lucy pointed out the fact that those phones cost the same no matter how many people were talked to, or for how long, so they might as well get some good out of them. She was a practical woman and generally frugal, though of late her income had risen to the point she had become more generous with herself. Her loom was now in the living room of the new house and she could talk and weave at the same time. But, she said, using her shoulder to hold the receiver was giving her a crick in her neck. Between the two of them they thought they had pretty much wormed out all the information their husbands knew concerning the recent murders. Suppositions still flew hot and heavy as the pair heated up the phone lines. One thing the women did not yet know was the latest on Luanne Keyoni's problems, and Charlie didn't intend for them to know either.

Sue heard Charlie's truck drive up, looked out the kitchen window and said, "Crap."

Three-year old Joseph Wiley also said "Cwap" though he didn't look up when he said it. He was pushing a plastic truck across the floor while listening to his mother talk, and had already added several new words to his vocabulary.

Sue Yazzie frowned down at him, but thought it counterproductive to say anything fearing it would only make things worse.

Charlie stopped to feed the horses, and by the time he came in, Sue was in a flurry of activity between the stove and sink.

"Running a little late here... Dinner in thirty minutes."

Charlie nodded and picked up his son. "Hey, buddy, how's that new truck working?"

"Cwap." Was all the boy could think to say about the truck.

Charlie looked across the kitchen at Sue. "Where'd he get that?"

"Beats me, maybe something on the TV. You should hear what some of these cartoon characters are saying these days, even makes me blush sometimes."

Charlie again nodded, thoughtfully this time, "Talked to Lucy Tallwoman today?"

"Oh, for just a minute. Can you watch this chorizo and eggs for a second? There's clothes in the washer and I need to get them out before I forget and they sour."

"Sure. Burritos for supper?" Charlie liked egg and chorizo burritos but thought they went better for breakfast than supper. He noticed the phone, slightly ajar on its cradle and put it to his ear; the earpiece was still warm but no one was on the line. The phone and the TV were a part of their lives now, a bigger part than Charlie had intended. The TV antenna had

116

taken him and Thomas Begay nearly a half-day to put up and they only got four channels, but two of the channels had cartoons in the afternoon and he felt there was no harm in letting Joseph Wiley watch a few from time to time.

Thomas had told them, "You're lucky, we only get two channels out at our house and only one has cartoons. The kids aren't happy about that. Harley doesn't get any channels... And Harley likes cartoons too."

When Sue came back to tend the dinner, Charlie got down on the floor with his son and showed him again how to operate the dump bed on his truck.

"So, anything new on those killings?" Sue tried to sound disinterested, just making conversation, but she turned one ear to catch his answer and was disappointed when he went on playing with the boy.

She was about to ask again but decided to wait. She knew she could push Charlie only so far. He was holding back something important. She was certain of it.

Charlie looked up and grinned. "I told you that was all privileged information. But no, there's really nothing new as yet."

"Well, Lucy Tallwoman says her father was in to see you this afternoon. What was that all about? She said Danny Hat's sister Luanne came out to their place yesterday, too, but that Paul wouldn't say what she wanted."

Charlie didn't look up this time, only said, "Hmmm," as he went on making an engine sound and pushing the toy truck around the floor. Joseph Wiley tried to make the sound as well but couldn't seem to get it right. Charlie looked at him a moment before turning toward the stove. "He can say 'crap' clear as a bell, but he can't make an engine noise?"

Sue shrugged, and began rolling burritos and stacking a platter. "Okay, it's ready, put him up at the table, and watch that highchair—that back leg you said you were going to fix is still wobbly, and it's getting worse too."

Charlie wiggled the chair back and forth before plopping the boy in it, then wiggled it again and said, "It's not bad. I'll try and get to it this weekend if I have time."

"Maybe if he falls out on his head you can find time." Sue didn't bother hiding her irritation.

Charlie looked across the table at her, took the saucer of scrambled egg and chorizo for Joseph Wiley's tray and barely caught the tortilla she tossed at him. "What's up? The washer didn't crap out again did it?"

Before Sue could answer, the baby grabbed up a handful of the burrito filling, held it out to Charlie and said, "Crap," clear as a bell.

"You see there! That's where he gets it!" Sue was on a roll and determined to get her husband's attention regardless of consequence.

Charlie calmly picked up a burrito and began eating, thinking his wife must have a good reason to be so out of sorts, it had been happening on a regular basis lately, but he couldn't fathom the cause of it. It just wasn't like her. *The last time this had happened was when she was pregnant and worried about witches and such.* She *had* been talking to Lucy Tallwoman a good bit lately, and he wondered if she had somehow gotten caught up in some new phase of her friend's more traditional life; some perceived threat perhaps. Sue would not have come to him with *that*, as she knew very well what his views on the subject were. That only left one other reason.

10

The Interrogation

Harley Ponyboy stared straight ahead but watched Charlie Yazzie from the corner of his eye and grew a little nervous as they drew closer to Luanne's place. Charlie had not said a whole lot for the last few miles but there was something in his manner that made Harley suspect he had reason to be upset with him.

At the camp Luanne shared with her mother and stepfather, there first seemed to be no one home. The only vehicle was a Ford truck that had obviously seen better days and had not been moved for a while.

Charlie stopped his truck a short distance from the hogan and looked past the brush arbor to the camp trailer. There was someone at the window Harley thought was Luanne. She came outside and fixed him with a steady gaze, which caused him to color as he hurried to get down from the Chevy. Charlie followed, and the three of them met in front of the summer hogan. The shelter had several gaps in the brush roof, and was in obvious need of repair. Luanne led them into the shade, where she indicated a derelict car seat opposite two kitchen chairs. She then stood with folded arms and waited for them to speak first.

Harley forced a smile. "How you been Luanne? Me and Charlie was just passing by and thought we would stop and talk a little. You probably already know Charlie's with Legal Services." He turned to the investigator. "He has a couple questions about Danny."

Luanne stood waiting and while she did not appear worried, she didn't seem happy to see them either.

Charlie cleared his throat and put on a smile. "Luanne, I see you now and then at the Co-op but you're generally too busy to talk."

"I'm busy right now." Luanne said as she moved to one of the chairs and sat down...and waited.

Charlie shrugged. "We'll only be a minute, just a few things I'd like to clear up...won't take a minute." He really hadn't taken much notice of Luanne these last few years and was surprised how she had aged. She was heavier now, looking tired and somewhat dark around the eyes. She had been quite a pretty girl when he'd first met her and it saddened him somehow to see her like this.

Luanne looked up at the brush roof as though taking note of the damage for the first time...maybe figuring what it might take to fix it. When she returned her gaze to the two she sounded irritated, "Billy Red Clay and the FBI were both out here already. Don't you guys talk? I don't know anything I haven't already told them." She looked down at her nearly new sneakers and bent to brush a piece of dried mud from one.

"Well, then maybe we can talk about you Luanne. Harley says you have a little problem left over from Danny's bigger problems." It wasn't what Charlie had meant to say, but it was close.

Harley shot a sharp glance at Charlie Yazzie and frowned, he hadn't expected this.

The woman looked thoughtfully over at Harley Ponyboy before turning back to the investigator, "I'm guessing you talked to Paul T'Sosi, too."

Charlie didn't bother denying this, instead brushed past it, "It's not like it's a secret, Luanne. People know what you and Danny were doing and have for some time—I didn't have to look far to find them either." Charlie's voice became gentler, "At this point we're more interested in getting you some help, than we are fixing blame. I'm not here to cause you trouble Luanne." He pointed toward Harley. "Harley here's like me, worried, and wants to do what's best for you. You've known Harley a long time...you know how he is."

Harley interrupted, "I didn't say nothin' Luanne." Then looked at Charlie in a way that caused the investigator a twinge of guilt.

Luanne took a deep breath, and when she let it out, her face relaxed and she closed her eyes as she nodded. "I don't know what more I can tell you that I haven't already said?"

"I'm interested in what you might have heard Danny say about a man named William Crawley? He's said to have come by the construction site from time to time...talked to Hoffman and James Erdric.

He may have something to do with a 'contract archaeology company,' clearing sites along the new highway." He paused and said, "Danny might have called them 'salvage operators' or some such a thing."

Luanne looked from one to the other trying to figure what they were really after, but finally nodded. "I don't recall Danny ever mentioning any William Crawley. But he did mention an archaeology outfit. He said they were not really a company at all. They were James Erdric's buyers for the things taken from the ruins. A 'fence' Danny called them. He said they were the money people. Danny wasn't part of that inner circle. He only did what Hoffman told him." She gave Harley a meaningful look before turning to Charlie. "I heard about that little set-to between Hoffman and Billy Red Clay." She stopped and a shudder ran through her. "Hoffman was a hard man––told Danny he would kill him if he ever talked to anyone about their business. That's probably why he didn't want Billy Red Clay to take him in." Her eyes filled. "Danny? He was in way over his head. He was scared to death our mother would catch wind of what he was doing...not just the drugs...but robbing what she calls, 'our ancestral sites.' My poor mother is convinced those people are our ancestors. She said she hears them calling for our help." Luanne grimaced. "She's big into Hopi religion...and politics, more so than when she was young. Her husband back then, Danny's father, was a secret member of some Indian rights group and fought for the Repatriation Act. She's been thinking about going back to the Hopi, maybe run for council even." She sniffed. "My father would never go to live with the Hopi. He's put up with plenty just for marrying her, he won't go."

"What do *you* think, Luanne? Are those people calling to you too?" Charlie couldn't help but wonder. *Was she torn between the two cultures like her mother?*

"Me? Naa, not me, or Danny neither, we didn't care one way or the other what happened to those ruins...or the people who built them. I don't think those people were anything like the Hopi are now."

Charlie sat back in his seat and didn't know what to think; Luanne needed help all right, maybe more than he'd first thought.

She saw what was going through his mind and standing up, looked down the road to the highway, "My mother and dad will be home from work any time now. I would rather you two not be here when they come." She gave a flip of her hair, "I'm tired of all these questions anyway. Nothing's going to bring Danny back."

Harley stood, suddenly anxious to be away, and waited until Charlie also came to his feet before saying, "Luanne, I'm really sorry we bothered you with this. It won't happen again." He gave Charlie a hard look, and with a push of his lips toward the truck, indicated it was time to go.

Charlie, still deep in thought, only nodded to Luanne as she was left standing in front of the arbor, not looking at them, but gazing beyond the mesas to some place she thought she'd rather be. Harley stood a moment, a little distance from the woman, trying to think of something to say that might help but couldn't. Charlie Yazzie was just hanging up the microphone when Harley climbed back in the truck and sat staring through the dirt streaked windshield.

~~~~~~

Harley Ponyboy and Charlie Yazzie were nearly to the Colorado line before either of them said a word. Charlie knew he had hurt his friend's feelings by putting him on the spot with Luanne. But felt he had only done what he thought was needed and didn't apologize.

The investigator was first to speak, "I'll do everything I can to see Luanne gets help." Charlie was not without influence when it came to the various tribal agencies, and intended to go out of his way for Luanne. He would do whatever he could.

Up until this point Harley had avoided looking at him, but now turned to regard the tribal investigator in a slightly different light. "That would be good, Charlie; she could use the help. She's a good person down deep. Her brother's death hit them all hard and it may take them a while to get over it."

Charlie looked up the road as they crossed what he thought might be the state-line. Someday, he figured there would be a sign to mark the place. Someone was always drawing lines across this country, dividing it up—making plats, and writing pieces of paper, deeds. All to prove ownership of something no one can own. No one owned this land in the beginning, and he doubted anyone would own it in the end. It would someday be as trackless and wild as when humans followed the first wooly mammoth across the Bering Straits. The professor was right;

there were no Native Americans, only immigrants, some earlier, some later, but immigrants all.

Those who came first claimed only what they could hold, either by tenacity, physical endurance, or by force of arms. That was how they came by these lands and later, how they lost them. When the Europeans came they called it "Manifest Destiny," a term they thought might justify the unjustifiable...if only to themselves. But it had been going on long before that, the strong displacing the weak, and in turn being displaced by others. Man has always wanted to brand things he covets, own them so to speak. Some things won't hold a brand. Charlie believed this wild country was one of those things.

"I guess were going on up to that Ute's place... Jimmy John, is it?" Harley thought it the wrong thing to do, but knew it was useless to say so.

"Yes, Jimmy John. There's something that didn't make sense that day James Erdric was killed. Jimmy John seemed way too anxious to please. Utes aren't known for cooperating with the authorities, and especially not with Navajo lawmen...at least that's been my experience."

"So what makes you think he's going to talk to you...on his own place, and in Colorado?"

"Oh, he'll talk to me all right... I'm almost sure of it."

Harley shook his head. "What makes you so sure?"

"Well I know a little something now...something I didn't know until I talked to Captain Beyale this morning. He'd sent for a record of Jimmy John's Colorado priors...there were several interesting similarities—not in the charges, but in the arrests themselves, now I know how to go about talking to him."

Charlie seemed to assume a different persona as he reached for his Stetson and pulled it down tight. "Sun's in my eyes." He said.

Jimmy John, along with several other men, was horseback, working a set of calves through a chute for inoculation and ear tags. The Ute saw Charlie's official truck coming from quite a distance and for just a moment it crossed his mind he ought to make a break for it. But he didn't, not in front of these younger relatives who still looked up to him. He was Uncle to two or three of them and they would think poorly of him if he ran.

Charlie circled his truck in behind the corrals and as he and Harley got out, the Indian cowboys sat silent on their horses watching them, waiting to see how Jimmy John would handle these out-of-state lawmen. Their uncle hesitated only a moment before getting down from his horse, then approached the truck with the hint of a swagger, making the cowboys think everything was all right and that Jimmy John of the Bear Clan had things under control.

The Ute knew who Charlie was, but couldn't imagine what he wanted. It might be as simple as a few innocuous questions, maybe ones he had already answered. He thought he'd handled that Navajo policeman, Hastiin Sosi, about right the day of the murder. Sosi had been lucky though. If this tribal investigator hadn't shown up when he did it might have been a whole different story for the officer. *This Yazzie fellow didn't even talk like an Indian.* No, he would have to think about this a little…but not too long.

When Charlie got out of the truck he pushed his hat back on his forehead and smiled at the pen of calves. "Those are a nice set of calves you boys have there…you must be running government bulls to make calves like those."

Now Jimmy was confused; this Law wasn't talking like a white man now, he seemed different somehow. "They're all right I guess…we buy our own bulls…from up in the Paradox," thinking everyone knew about the bulls raised in the Paradox Valley. He didn't intend to spar around with a Navajo cop who had no authority in Colorado.

"Well, they look good." Charlie smiled, "You must get a little more rain up this way." He pushed his chin at the loafing shed at the side of the corrals. "You wouldn't have someplace we can talk, would you, Jimmy?" The other men had gone back to working the calves and Charlie kept his eye on Jimmy as he spoke to Harley over his shoulder. "Harley can you stay by that radio? I'm expecting a call from Agent Mayfield. He's on his way up here and might need directions. You can just toot the horn if he calls."

Harley looked a little confused at this, but turned back to the truck.

Jimmy John nodded toward the shed, but was unsmiling, and more than a little apprehensive that the FBI might be on the way. He had already been questioned by the FBI man and thought he was all right there…now this. As he led the way into the loafing shed he rolled these things around in his mind and quickly came to the conclusion this Navajo was bluffing…that or he was being set up.

The Ute wasn't tall but he was built like a tractor and Charlie took that into account. The shed was open in front but inside they were out of sight of the cowboys…and of Harley.

When Jimmy John turned and started to say something, Charlie's fist caught him full in the mouth; still the Ute didn't go down, which was disappointing, but he *was* stunned and his head listed slightly to the side. Charlie hit him again, this time in the nose and something popped. Thomas often said, "There is something about a broken nose that will take the fight out of most men." Jimmy went to one knee with blood gushing, which in itself has a certain psychological value.

Charlie had been in a few fights, but mostly when he was young. He had never been very good at it and could see now he had been going about it all wrong. Having seen Thomas Begay put men away over the years it had been impressed upon him that taking the first shot was important. Thomas had always been first and then never let up—that was the second most important thing—you don't ever let up. Thomas had mentioned how important that was.

If Captain Beyale had not sent him the Ute's rap sheet he could not have known of the assaults on previous arresting officers, and then it might have been *him* on the ground with a bloody nose. As Charlie stood over the man he was surprised to find himself fully prepared to kick him in the face, should the Ute be so foolish as to try getting up. He knew for certain it's what Thomas Begay would do. He had never felt that urge before, but it was on him now and he intended to act on it should he have to.

"Jimmy, I'm going to ask you this...just one time...then I'm going to get mean with you." His voice took on an ominous tone and he sounded like a dangerous person, even to himself. "You've got a key to that trailer where Erdric died...don't you?"

The Ute shook his head and Charlie drew back a foot, but when the Ute cowered and raised his hand to wave him off he hesitated a moment as a tremor ran through the downed man.

"That trailer was where I stayed...before Erdric took it over...like he did everything else." Jimmy John was holding his nose together and his voice was muffled and weak. There was no more fight left in him.

"And you took the turquoise amulet he had on him there in the trailer, too, didn't you—the one Erdric stole from the ruins?" Charlie had known when he saw the matching beads by the body that James Erdric had the amulet. It hadn't shown up in the FBI report, so it must have been taken before the tribal policeman arrived on the scene.

Jimmy John hesitated, started to deny it, but thought better of it as he saw Charlie yet again draw back his boot. He nodded, groaned, and sat back, hands to his nose, gently probing, trying to push it back into some semblance of its former self. Charlie reached in his back pocket, removed a set of handcuffs and secured the man to a nearby feed bunk.

"I didn't shoot him you know," Jimmy John's mouth was so swollen Charlie had trouble understanding him. Seeing this, the Ute reiterated, "I did not...shoot...him!"

"The FBI's looking into that right now; I guess we'll know soon enough." Charlie moved to the front of the building and motioned for Harley to bring the pickup. The FBI agent should already be on his way and could make the actual arrest then transport the Ute across the state line. Charlie smiled, Mayfield thought he was coming to question Jimmy John in lieu of some new evidence, but would soon find the questioning already done and that he need only re-cover the amulet, and return the prisoner to New Mexico in Federal custody.

11

1075 A.D.

Together

The village was larger now with a few more second-story rooms built by the newcomers. Others moved to close in the far end of the alcove, adding storage and living quarters. In the spring they would begin a new *kiva* just for themselves; they had been builders in the old town to the south and proven craftsmen. The boy thought the elders had been wise to allow these people to join them.

Not far into winter the boy's new wife suffered the death of her father and he was buried in the deep drift at the back of the alcove. Her mother, and the orphan girl found along the trail, lived together then, and with only a little help from the community took care of one another. The mother was a skilled potter and was teaching the girl the craft, just as she had her own daughter. The youngster was an apt pupil and already did credible work for one her age. Most of what they made was stored away as dry clay vessels, waiting for spring, when fuel could be gathered and the process completed through firing. They would be ceramics then, and they, or some part of them, might last forever.

The boy's father and sister were only two rooms away. The old man, too, was failing, and the boy's wife had taken up the burden of caring for the girl. The two were of an age and like-minded. His sister took a great liking to her brother's new wife, and thought her being "Swallow Clan" a good omen. The two confided in one another and each learned things known only to the other. The sister saw in the young wife what she herself might have been, but was not jealous or ill disposed toward her on that account. As winter deepened the helpless girl grew listless and weak, but still the elders came to seek her advice, were pleased with what they heard and her position among them grew ever stronger. Her brother became her voice at council and thus he, too, gained importance. His words were well spoken and listened to as those of an older, wiser person.

The harsh winter storms were thought by some to be a harbinger of a wetter spring, and that brought hope. Perhaps the Gods were listening now and their prayers would bring more bountiful crops and easier times. There would be people enough now to work on the dams and ditches, whatever rain might come their way could be saved and meted out to the fields. There were turkeys in the upper reaches of the side canyons and in the spring, when they nested, boys could be sent to watch from hiding, and as the young birds hatched they could be caught and brought back to be raised in the village. There would be feathers for blankets then, and eggs for both young and old.

Tamed turkeys were seldom eaten...wild ones were hunted for that. If only the rains returned, life could be good again. Perhaps then women who had remained barren through lack of food and too much hard work would conceive, and again the sound of children would lighten the hearts of the people. All that was in the future and still in the hands of the Gods. For now, wolves were foremost in their minds. The elders worried and their dreams were troubled. The boy, who was now a man, remained ever on his guard, rising before the sun each morning to watch the trails below the little tower and make certain there were no fresh tracks in the snow. There had been no sign of the wolves since the latest storms and he thought the weather might be keeping them close to their fires.

His people had only two dogs left but if they didn't have to eat them there would be more in the spring. These were smaller dogs, good hunters, and in better times mostly fended for themselves. They were kept close now to sound an alarm should strangers approach. No one begrudged them what few scraps they stole from the cook fires.

The boy knew, eventually, the winds would turn and come from the south as they almost always did in midwinter; that would bring a thaw. Then the wolves would return to haunt them. The newcomers said the raiding parties seldom numbered more than a dozen––only a third of village numbers—but the raiders were hardened warriors...and desperate.

It had been his father who proposed the great slab of rock be placed just at the entrance to the village. It had taken six men, with poles to raise it enough to lean against the overhang in such a fashion as to allow only a narrow passage into the village. In the wide space, just inside, a lesser piece of sandstone was slid into place in front of the entrance. It took three strong men to move it in front of the passage. On the other side of the barricade the trail was so narrow as to allow only one person at a time to approach—certainly not enough to force entry. No one had seen a village so secure from attack. As long as they could stay in the alcove they would be safe. A small seep at the back of the alcove might, with careful management, provide enough water for drinking, and snow could be melted. Nonetheless, a foraging party must eventually be sent to gather firewood and hunt what little game had migrated from the high country. Even then, he knew, the wolves would be waiting.

It was in the coldest part of the middle month of winter that the old people read portents in the clouds and eagerly awaited the breezes, almost warm, wafting up the canyon from the south. This was the way of these Chinooks. They came just as the wild creatures were on their last legs and even the people thought they could stand no more. It was almost as though they were being tested and then finally awarded a reprieve.

The younger people preferred to think it an early spring and that the worst was over. Older and wiser heads knew this was not the case—it might last only a few days... a week at the most, and they had best make the most of it. When winter returned it would come fierce and unrelenting, and torture them for at least another month, maybe two. This was but a respite and their lives might well depend on how they took advantage of it. Firewood was nearly gone and there had been no meat for many weeks. Even the dogs came under the calculating gaze of the elders, and were now relieved not to suffer those hungry looks. The dogs did not belong to any one person, but to everyone and probably, in the end, that was what saved them.

In the council, on the second night of the thaw, the elders debated the wisdom of sending out a foraging party. In the midst of the many uncertainties there were, as usual, a few weak and dissenting voices, but finally all conceded there could be no other choice. A small band of their strongest must leave the safety of the village and secure what was needed. Nearly all the capable males volunteered to go and were excited at the prospect—the young ones thinking it a chance for adventure, possibly even glory. Some thought any lurking raiders would surely take advantage of the thaw to move south to more favorable prospects and probably not present any real danger. The boy warrior chosen to lead knew better. He said they were wrong. His past experience led him to believe the outliers would first wait to see what opportunities were available close by before moving south. He knew they would be unrelenting when once they set their sights. The wolves would not let them off so easily as that. It was only through his success in the battle to the north, that he was able to convince every volunteer that they went at the risk of their lives and probably of those they left behind as well. Two older men then dropped out saying they would stay to help protect those left behind. They were farmers, too old they said, and best left at home.

The leader studied them all, several younger than himself, and of the more than dozen volunteers, agreed two of them were too old. Even his father had wanted to join with them but was refused on the grounds he hadn't the stamina to keep up with the others. Should these men meet with no evil at the hands of a raiding party, they still might come back loaded with wood enough to at least keep the *kiva* fire burning and perhaps enough meat, when stewed with corn and beans, to last through the worst times. While it would be easy going down the canyon, it would be much harder coming back and the volunteers were carefully chosen for that reason. Should it come to a fight he felt only three or four were likely to give a good account of themselves and that, only if they could gain the upper hand at the start. These men were thin, but strong and rested. He wondered if the same could be said of the wolves a larger breed and relentless in the chase, though they had been long on the trail, exposed to the elements, and probably with little to eat.

The boy decided not to bring the dogs, even though some thought they might be put to good use in the hunt. He argued against this and said he thought they were better left in the village to warn of enemies should they become desperate enough to attempt an attack. There were only old men and women left to fend off those more seasoned warriors. Some of the women were probably more capable than the old men they must fight alongside, and even though the village was thought impregnable, one never knew what sort of trickery these wild people might come up with. They too, had their ways.

"No," he told them, "The dogs are best left in the village."

A young man of the newcomers agreed, and said things might have been different for his own village should they have had dogs to warn them. Their dogs, he said, had taken sick from eating a coyote and died. The few who had wanted to take the dogs relented, seeing the wisdom in the leader's advice, and his position grew stronger, all now satisfied he was the right choice to lead.

It was a more serious group that slid back the stone slab that night and ventured forth with the somber thought it might be the last some of them saw of their home. The people who remained watched the little band disappear down the narrow cliff-side trail, and held similar thoughts.

It was only six or seven hours hard travel to the cedar breaks below, where they should find ample dead wood and perhaps even deer or desert sheep. It had been a long time since there had been meat.

Just before their canyon ran into the larger low-land basin, they halted. A good hunter was sent ahead to wait for dawn, scout what game there might be, and any sign of enemies. The more optimistic hoped to find tracks of the marauders heading south to prey on smaller, less protected settlements, thereby leaving their village in peace.

An hour after dawn the scout returned with news of deer in the oak brush below the cedar draws. There was just enough snow, he said, to make tracking easy. This was good news and the best hunters were sent ahead so as not to frighten the animals with the sound of the wood gatherers' stone axes.

The leader took the scout side and asked if he found any sign of enemies. The man shook his head, threw a worried glance back the way they had come, and said, "No, they did not leave this country before us. They are still back there, possibly at the village as far as I can see." The man was known to be a thorough and skilled tracker; there was little chance he was wrong. There were only two possibilities. The interlopers had watched them go and the village might already be under attack; or they were waiting to ambush the heavily laden party on their return and then lay siege to the village.

Within hours the hunters killed a buck fattened on acorns and piñon nuts, then butchered it for packing. They set to work picking the best and densest wood, breaking it into short lengths to be packed on their backs with tumplines about their foreheads. In the fall they had girdled many trees closer to the village, but those were not yet ready, Green wood would not be easy to break into firewood with stone axes, and all the easy wood had already been gathered, much of it within months of when they first arrived. Until the wolves moved on...or were confronted, it would be dangerous, and foolish, to fell timber and break it up with enemies watching.

The foragers did not rest or wait for morning and again left under cover of darkness. Loaded as heavily as they dared they started for home with the breeze still blowing fresh from the south—temperatures mild in comparison to those they recently endured. They intended to avoid the lower canyon trail and take the long way around to approach the village from above. This, the boy thought was their only chance to avoid ambush.

12

Sands of Time

Professor George Armstrong Custer was not one to take lightly a threat against his livelihood, and when Harley Ponyboy told him Charlie Yazzie was making inquiries into the business of archaeologist William Crawley, he immediately evinced a strong interest in those findings. He had already been suspicious of Crawley's involvement in the newly formed salvage company, and based on what FBI Agent Mayfield had hinted, now believed Crawley to be the person the agent had been referring to in their last conversation. He had long been aware of rumors out of Guatemala linking Crawley to the disappearance of a coworker thought to be working undercover for the Guatemalan government.

Now three men were dead, and George Custer believed the situation serious enough to buy himself a revolver. He began wearing it even when wielding a shovel in the confines of the dig. Thomas Begay was quick to pick up on this, and asked Charlie Yazzie if he could borrow his .38 Smith. He said he didn't want to depend on the professor's limited expertise to protect him and Harley, should it ever come to that. And clearly, the professor seemed to consider it a possibility.

"No, I don't think so," the investigator replied after only a moment.

"Why not?"

"Well, for one thing the gun is registered to me, and if you should feel called on to use deadly force—I can see that happening—it would most likely come back on me."

"How about if I tried to only wing someone with it?"

"No!"

Thomas hadn't really expected Charlie to let go of the gun, but thought he might at least refuse in a more considerate manner.

Charlie didn't care what Thomas thought. He felt the situation spiraling out of control since the arrest of the Ute, Jimmy John, who remained in FBI custody in Farmington. The man was currently held on antiquities charges, but prosecutors hinted at something much more serious, murder, being a distinct possibility.

These were just a few of the things occupying the professor's mind that morning as he worked to uncover the kiva burial. Harley Ponyboy stood nearby, and looked on with interest as Dr. Custer wielded what he called his "micro trowel" along the edge of the shredded cedar bark lining the pit. At this stage of the excavation the professor took over from his assistant, and it became Harley's job to hand him various instruments of the trade, including a small short bristled paintbrush, and the professor's own worn-out toothbrush brought in a shirt pocket just that morning.

No matter how many burials the archaeologist uncovered, each new one was as exciting as the first. No one knew what would be uncovered, or what information might for the first time, cast light on some question whose answer was previously only guessed at. To think he would soon view something not seen by human eyes in nearly a thousand years was pure magic—an excitement he could not suppress, or explain to anyone who had no passion for the science and mystery involved.

A layer of windblown dust and sand was delicately brushed aside, and added to the plastic bin that would later be screened for tiny artifacts that might provide additional clues. Already there had been several more turquoise beads recovered, of the same type associated with the turquoise amulet, now considered evidence by the FBI.

When a narrow perimeter had been meticulously channeled around the burial, the professor could see the whole of the thing was nearly intact. Due to the eons of desiccating conditions in the alcove he suspected the remains might well be mummified, a rare find indeed. The information learned from a burial in such a state of preservation might offer valuable clues to the culture.

Several ceramic vessels of an unusually high quality could be seen at the side of the burial and these, along with the previously found amulet, caused the professor to think this the grave of an unusually important person. He wished Charlie Yazzie could be there to see this, he was certain now it was no ordinary burial.

Thomas waited at the edge of the kiva with the long plastic container used to transport remains from the field. The professor looked up and shook his head.

"We won't be needing that just yet, Thomas." Dr. Custer seemed deep in thought as he began gently laying back the wrappings, the first covering a loosely woven reed sleeping mat. The professor had often excavated remains that still carried a moldy or even fetid odor—even after the passage of hundreds of years. But this burial had virtually no odor, even after the second cover had been exposed; a blanket of turkey feathers woven with narrow strips of rabbit fur, thick and full even now. It would have been warm, but lightweight, with the ability to breath, yet insulate. The protected nature of the storage bin had indeed allowed preservation to an unusual degree. The feather and fur blanket was soft, supple and nearly free of insect or rodent damage.

Kivas were not ordinarily known to harbor burials and especially not in these Chaco-linked villages. Remarkably few burials of any kind had turned up in the great towns of the Chaco Canyon. It was still not known why this was so, or how this particular group of Anasazi disposed of their dead; another ancient mystery modern science had, as yet, been unable to unravel.

The professor took his time now, pondering each step and from time to time, made notes and diagrams in his field journal. He asked Thomas to pass down his old Graflex; a veteran of many archaeological adventures, then took several shots of each stage of the exhumation. Custer judged the light and shutter speed by dint of long experience, but still took the precaution of bracketing exposures, some at least, might be exactly right. He set the camera aside finally, and carefully lifted the blanket to see the mummified remains of what was obviously a young woman, dressed in a deerskin skirt and cloak so finely tanned and sewn as to appear recently made. It was apparent the person had sustained serious injury at some early stage of her life, lower limbs wasted and probably useless. She was draped with several strings of tiny turquoise and shell beads. Many burials of men had been found displaying funerary dress and offerings of this caliber, but not many women had been afforded such consideration.

This was not the first evidence the professor had found showing the Anasazi's compassion in providing long-term care for disabled victims of accident or disease. Broken bones and serious injury from falls or rock slides were not uncommon among these people. There were even known examples of attempted surgeries, including the trepan of skulls to alleviate swelling of the brain, incredibly, a few patients apparently survived the ordeal…at least for a while. Splinting of broken bones was common, and some of these healed almost perfectly.

Someone had gone to a great deal of trouble to send this young person on her last journey in so fine a manner, despite her obvious inability to contribute to the community in a more physical way, the professor couldn't help but wonder, *Was there some more intangible gift or service she was able to offer in return?* It was probably the comparative security earned through agriculture, and its sedentary lifestyle that allowed so strong a devotion. The itinerate existence of the early wandering tribes would have made this level of attachment impossible.

~~~~~~

Charlie Yazzie sat entranced at his kitchen table as Thomas Begay and Harley Ponyboy related the recent discovery in minute detail, embellishing the story with their own thoughts and conclusions as they went along.

"There weren't any evil hanging over this dead person, at least as far as Harley and me could feel."

Harley agreed, "She seemed so comfortable there the professor decided to leave her "in situ." The words were becoming a favorite of the little man and Charlie had to smile as he gave a quick lift of an eyebrow in Thomas's direction, who, grinned in turn and punched Harley's shoulder but in a friendly way.

The tribal investigator was pleased to see his friends less intimidated by the dead: he thought it showed promise of things to come. He gave the professor credit for helping with that transformation, but doubted it would affect their fear of their own people's dead; that was a matter of *chindi,* and it might never go away. In the far reaches of his mind he was not so certain he was immune to it himself.

The professor arrived late in the afternoon, the three Navajo already at the corrals. Harley was to do a little hoof trimming in return for a haircut and some laundry. There seems to be a magnetic attraction between the *Diné* and corrals. They gather there regardless of what animals might be held in the enclosure and, if there are none, they discuss what could be acquired to fill them. An empty corral is an affront to the sensibilities not many can ignore, and the urge to do something about it can entail long and sometimes heated discussions. In this particular case, however, there were two horses to hold their attention. Horses have long been a favorite subject of Indian conversation, and they are still of vital interest to many.

One can ride horses or race them…or use them to rope or herd. They can be bought, sold or bartered, and those possibilities make for endless debate.

The professor recalled, only a few years back, how one could sit in any restaurant or gas station on the reservation and see people who showed a slight limp or lacked the full use of an arm or hand. Many of these anomalies were attributable to horse-related incidents, including missing thumbs from roping mishaps. Women, and children too, were avid riders and apt to incur various injuries as well, though not as many as was once the case.

Sue watched from the clotheslines as she hung Harley's wash. The dryer was already full, and he had mentioned he preferred to have his Levis dried outside. He thought the dryer was shrinking them, he said, though Sue could see he was just gaining weight.

Joseph Wiley, even at three years old, ran back and forth along the fenced in yard and yelled for his father to come for him so he could go see the horses. Charlie looked up from the corrals and waved but didn't move to fetch the boy.

Professor Custer moved alongside the Tribal Investigator as they watched Harley catch up Sue's mare and walk her around to see how she stood, and how best to do her feet.

"I guess the boys told you all about the burial in the Kiva?" The professor asked with a smug smile.

"Yes they did, and I have to say I'm surprised you've decided to leave her in place and not ship her off to the lab for evaluation. You've always said there was a lot to be learned from such burials."

"I don't know, Charlie, there's just something about this entire situation...the murders and all, that makes me think it best we just fill in the kiva and let it be for now."

So unscientific a view was out of character for the professor and though surprised, Charlie nodded and felt justified in the high regard in which he had always held George Custer. "Well, she'll always be there I suppose, George, should you ever change your mind...at least I hope she'll be there."

"I'm working on that. A local historical society has agreed to fund an eight-foot-high chain link fence to secure the alcove from passers-by. It will still leave the buildings viewable from the new road, yet for the most part, inaccessible." The professor gave a grim shake of his head. "Nothing's forever Charlie; we can only do what we can do. We'll backfill the Kiva with rubble and hopefully that alone will deter digging. I've already charted several more suspected burials in the back of the alcove, which haven't been disturbed. I'll have most of the data written up pretty soon, so I'm thinking it's time to wrap this one up." He leaned on the top rail of the corral to watch Harley tie the mare to the snubbing post and lay his nippers and rasp out on the ground.

The professor murmured under his breath, "Like you say Charlie, I know where she is."

Charlie Yazzie changed the subject. "We should have final word from the federal prosecutor's office sometime in the next day or so, about charges the maintenance man, Jimmy John, might be liable for. They've been pretty closemouthed; that makes me think they are making a case against him in the murder of James Erdric." Charlie frowned before going on, "Captain Beyale said Agent Mayfield has had his people working nonstop."

Professor Custer lowered an eyelid and looked askance at this news. Do they even know where Erdric was when he was shot?"

"Not yet, but they do know it wasn't long after being hit that he made it to the trailer and locked himself inside. His truck was found in its usual parking place just outside the camp and with no sign it had even been used that night. The FBI figured he was shot somewhere else."

Thomas Begay was now in the corral, feeling it best he just hold the mare himself rather than leave her tied to the post. She was still a little green when it came to her feet, and he didn't want her to jerk back and maybe hurt herself. He had helped break this mare for Sue and had told her the horse still had some spook left in her. He kept an eye on the professor and Charlie, wondering what sort of conversation could cause them to look so serious.

Charlie turned and glanced a time or two at the horse trimming, then directed his attention back to the professor. "Funny thing is, the FBI doesn't seem to think the gunshot wound was serious enough to kill him—turns out what we thought were knife wounds, *were* knife wounds, and one severed an artery near his heart. That's what killed him."

"So someone killed him after he locked himself in the trailer? That doesn't make any sense."

Charlie didn't change expression when he answered, "It makes perfect sense, if someone had a key and was right behind him."

"The Ute?"

"Looks that way. I can't tell you more right now, Doc, but between you and me I would say it's a safe bet that Jimmy John's going down for this one."

"Do they think he killed Hoffman too?"

"Hoffman's another matter—I'll let you know when I hear more on it, but I can tell you right now, that's a whole different can of worms."

Harley had one of the mare's feet tucked up between his knees and he and the horse were doing a little dance despite Thomas keeping her head up.

"If you can't hold her," Harley yelled, "Just say so and we'll tie her back up ta that post...I know that'll hold her." Harley was stout but he could no longer hold onto the foot and released the mare then jumped aside and threw down his nippers in a huff. "I don't know why you untied her in the first place. She was doing okay just as she was." Harley and Thomas often disagreed when it came to horses and it looked like this was going to be another one of those times.

Charlie and the professor broke off their conversation at the row in the corral, and Charlie moved toward the gate hoping to get the trimming session back on track. " Give her a minute, Harley; let her settle down a bit."

"No, if I do that, she's gonna' start thinking she's won and that means we will have ta go through the whole thing again. I better just stick with her on this." This turned out to be something Thomas and Harley both agreed on and Charlie was voted down.

Sue called down from the yard, "Let them do what they want Charlie!" then whispered under her breath, "You're not the one doing the trimming Charlie." She thought *why does he have to interfere? Thomas and Harley both know their way around a horse, and just because Charlie's grandfather was a horse trainer doesn't make him one.* Sue was fast getting in a state. She scooped up her toddler and headed for the house before she said something she might be sorry for later. Her husband looked after her and it was the sort of look that made Thomas Begay uneasy as he turned to consider them. It took Harley Ponyboy some time to finish with the horses but even Thomas admitted it was a good job and he made the thumbs up sign to Charlie and the professor. Charlie appeared not to notice, glancing occasionally at the house and mouthing words no one could hear.

Sue peered from the kitchen window at the little gathering at the corral and felt a twinge of guilt... She should tell Charlie.

13

1075 A.D.

The Wolves

The little band of foragers made slow progress despite being accustomed to hard going. In the lowlands, the Chinook winds reduced snow to a freezing slush, making the trail even slicker and harder to climb with the heavy packs. A full moon made the path easier to follow, but once they left the main trail the way to the mesa top would become steeper and the wet snow would turn to ice; still it would all be worth it to avoid the almost certain ambush should they return the way they came.

It was while they stopped to catch their breath the tracker returned with bad news. The wolves were on to them. He had found signs of a scout on their back trail, only one man, but sent to follow them. The spy was keeping well back, and off the main trail—had probably been there from the beginning, and most likely still was. The tracker suggested he should fall back, lie in wait—kill him if he could, before their new strategy was reported. He was a young man filled with visions of glory. Should he succeed in eliminating this danger his name would surely be spoken in council. Perhaps then he, too, could sit with the elders. The leader knew his young friend, like himself, was more a warrior at heart than a farmer, and there was a good chance he could stop this new threat. In any case, they now had little choice in the matter. The wolves must not know they were going home the back way across the mesa. Returning the way they had come would surely mean a battle…and one they might not win.

When they finally angled up and away from the main trail for the climb out to the mesa top, the scout still had not returned. The leader hesitated, waited as long as he dared, then pressed on. They must reach the village before daylight: too many lives were at stake to linger in the cause of one man. Though all were heavily loaded, each kept a weapon at hand, ready to drop his pack and defend himself at a moment's notice. Their village could not fend off an attack for very long without them, and should that be the way of it, they were prepared to die in the effort.

The snow grew deeper at this higher elevation, the way more arduous, and there was a growing worry the man left behind to secure their back-trail, still had not caught up. They were nearly to the top when they paused to rest and, in the icy moonlit silence a faraway cry was heard. It could only be the tracker, perhaps wounded and unable to catch up. The leader immediately dropped his pack and instructed the others to go on while he went back to see what had become of the scout. He carried his bow and a dozen arrows in the quiver slung across his back. The moon was bright, and reflected by the snow, allowed him to see a good distance down the trail. He became more cautious as he worked his way through the scant cover, pausing to stop now and again to study the way ahead. When he came to a small clearing he saw a dark form huddled at the base of a juniper. With an arrow nocked and ready, he eased forward, keeping to the trees above the path, and alert to the very core of his being. He stepped behind a snow-covered piñon and watched through the heavy branches. He didn't move, remained perfectly still and watched. Minutes passed, he grew stiff from the cold yet remained within his cover, *Something is not right,* he thought to himself, then sensed, more than saw, the flicker of movement at the far edge of the trees.

He doubted he had been seen or he would already be shot. He was well within bow range and knew, should he give himself away by changing position, he would be equally vulnerable. It was then he remembered the rescue of his wife, and the hoot of an owl used by the raider's sentry. Should this one be of those same people, he might catch him off guard by such a call. Slowly, he drew his bow to its full reach then made the sound of a hunting owl, concentrating on the place he thought he'd seen movement. The dark form under the tree surprised him by rising to one knee to extend his head and revealing his wolf-skin hood.

The leader let fly the arrow and heard the faint thud of a body hit. Without moving from the spot he nocked yet another arrow and waited. Only when he heard the deep rattle of a lung shot did he move, keeping brush and trees between him and the dying spy. As he crept closer he could see the man was as good as dead, and cautiously continued toward the place he thought he had last seen movement. His friend lay at the base of a tree, shot twice; the last a solid hit. The first cry probably escaped him when he was shot the first time…or the call had been from the wolf—cunning and quick to deceive as were all his tribe. The killer knew he could not be far behind the foraging party and possibly thought to lure someone to the aid of the dying tracker. The man's cloak hung in a tree to move in the breeze and, if only for an instant, be a distraction. This spy was skilled…and deadly but the raiders would never know his fate or where he lay. The villagers would come back in the spring to bury this clansman he must now leave behind.

Daylight was only hours away and he jogged up the ridge, to recover his pack and follow the others. The party left a clear path for him to follow, making his way faster. He was sure now that he would catch them before daylight. There might still be a chance to reach the village unchallenged.

The first grey lines of dawn outlined the mesa to the east and the wind, previously from the south, began clocking around to the west, then to the north. The temperature dropped and the trail turned to ice. Loaded with meat and wood the way down would make for treacherous work, and if they didn't hurry, the coming dawn would make them easy targets on the cliff's narrow trail.

~~~~~

The wolves were waiting for word from their spy before moving on the settlement. They posted an additional lookout down-canyon. This should allow enough warning to reposition their ambush if necessary. Being caught between the returning foragers and those left guarding the village might be a fatal mistake. The alcove was a difficult bowshot from their place in the canyon—but not so hard from the villagers vantage above; that had to be taken into account.

The original plan was to bide their time and figure some way to get past the blocked entrance. They could see now that might come at a heavy price. Should the provisions make it through to bolster the cliff dwellers' morale, further attempts at dislodging them would probably prove futile. Then they would have to move on and hope for easier prey. That way would take them south and farther from their own country. Whatever spoils they might gain would be hard to transport north to those who remained on the brink of starvation.

They could not wait too long for a chance at these little people who lived high in the rocks and defended their homes so fiercely. If the sentry down-canyon brought word of the foraging party's return they would lie in wait, take them by surprise in the depths of the canyon. They might then have provisions enough to wait out these villagers left with no hope of rescue.

Just as the boy finally caught up with his companions, the breaking dawn brought a glow to the treetops along the edge of the mesa. At the rim the foragers readjusted their loads for the dangerous descent. The moon fell behind the distant mountains, leaving the canyon shrouded in mists rising from the void, still dark, and in shadows. The boy did not mention the fate of their tracker, but the others sensed the worst, and looked down into the foreboding darkness with growing doubt. Even in good weather it was not an easy trail down, with the ice it seemed impossible. Still hidden in shadow, and out of bow-range from below, they could not be targeted until crossing the narrow trail to the alcove. Though the lower reaches of the canyon lay in darkness they knew eyes were watching, waiting, for that first glimpse of someone on the trail above.

~~~~~~~

From the small lookout tower the young wife also watched the trail skirting the face of the cliff. When she heard the rattle of pebbles thrown down to the alcove as a warning, she signaled to the little girl down below. The foraging party had returned and she must alert those in the *kiva* to come slide back the stone, and prepare themselves for battle should it come to that. Those called on to fight this day would surely be remembered for many generations…should any be left to tell of it.

~~~~~~~

In the first glimmer of dawn, the wolves' lookout discovered the ruse; knew the foraging party had tricked them by coming across the mesa. Now the raiders' only hope was to catch the heavily loaded men as they started across the rock face. They must hurry to fall in behind them on the trail—pick off the heavily loaded foragers one by one as they reached that dangerously narrow section before the alcove. A villager would pull back the stone slab and if the wolves were quick they might force their way in. They were bigger and stronger than these little people, and even more desperate. The foragers' unexpected arrival from above might be more of an opportunity than they first imagined and they now intended to make the most of that opportunity.

The lingering darkness sheltered the foraging party coming in from the top, but offered even more protection for the raiders in the deep shadows of the canyon. They gave themselves over to instinct, doing what wolves do best, moving cautiously, pausing often to listen for the slightest movement…anything that might signal the approach of the descending party. They must wait and catch the returning party stretched out ahead of them on the icy and treacherous trail across the cliff. Should dawn catch the wolves on their way up and in view of the alcove it might go badly for them. They learned the hard way to avoid going below the alcove—only the day before they approached too near hoping to shoot arrows into the village. The defenders had prepared for just such an attack, staying just out of sight, the women and old men rained down stones on the interlopers, and quickly drove them away. One of the wolves suffered a broken arm, leaving them short yet another fighting man.

The spy originally sent to follow the foragers and report back had still not returned and they were certain now he had been intercepted. That tracker had been the best of their warriors and the very one who tracked these people to their nest. He felt certain it was these farmers who had wiped out some of their fiercest warriors only months before. When their bodies were discovered it was first not believed possible. The sign showed no more than two of these farmers had killed them. This stirred a frenzy that led the wolves to rampage south, leaving terrible devastation in their wake. The settlements were shown no mercy, nor were prisoners taken; the last thing they needed were more mouths to feed.

Their injured man was sent to an overlook where he discovered there were only women and old men left. With a little luck they would wreak a deadly reckoning on these farmers.

When finally they heard the first of the descending foragers, cautiously edging their way down the steep and icy path, the leader of the wolves turned with an upraised finger, signing the party must be allowed out on the narrowest part of the trail before moving in for the kill. The heavily laden farmers would be unable to turn and fight. There could be no mistake this time…there would be no second chance.

~~~~~~

On the mesa's rim it was decided the three men who carried the packs of venison should go first, followed by those with the bulkier loads of wood which might be less manageable on the worst of the trail. They would have left the wood behind at the top but knew how badly it was needed for the *kiva,* where all might take some comfort from it in the coming weather. Should something make this impossible the wood haulers were instructed to release their loads, letting them fall to the bottom of the cliff, where they might later be recovered. Their leader left his load at the top, so he might better provide cover for the others. When he reached a switchback he knew would allow a view of the cliff-face, he stopped and prepared to defend his companions at all cost.

Daybreak came slowly, creeping over the rim to penetrate the mist shrouded nooks and crannies. The boy could not see the lower trail, and only bits and pieces of the upper trail. The boy *could* see across to the village, the stone barrier still in place. He was sure his young wife had been watching and heard their earlier signal; there would be people prepared to move the stone slab blocking the entrance. He was certain the wolves would be on them at first light and only a great familiarity with the trail allowed his own men to move ahead in near darkness. His people had a reputation for their agility on these rocky canyon ledges, but even they had second thoughts, especially those with bundles of wood that might catch on an overhang and send the packer to the bottom.

Three of the first four were nearly to the stone barrier, already being pushed aside. An old man, known to have been very good with a bow, had taken a position in the little guard tower alongside the boy's wife. She stationed herself beside a pile of stones and was prepared to use them. She heard her husband's shouted warning as the first of the raiders emerged from hiding and sent an arrow among the helpless group on the trail. It was a long shot and the arrow fell short, striking the load of wood carried by the fourth in line. In an instant that man slipped out of his tumpline and edged the pack against the wall, using it as a precariously balanced shield. He eased his bow from the side of the pack and prepared to send an arrow in return but could see nothing in the distant shadows.

The old man watching from the tower spotted the attacker and sent an arrow his way. The range was hard to judge in the early dawn and his missile, too, was low, but caught that warrior in the knee, enough to put him off balance. Although a hand was seen to reach out to him, the man tumbled off the ledge to the rocks below. The wood hauler, behind his pack, loosed his arrow at the dark space where the hand reached out. There was a faint yelp on the wind but the shooter could not know what had come of his effort. He did not dare push the bundle of wood off the ledge. That would leave him defenseless, the man knew it would be only a matter of seconds until another wolf took the place of the first. The three men with the more manageable packs of venison were nearly to the barrier when the first was hit low in the back yet stumbled toward the now open entrance to the village. He was nearly there when hit again, this time in the lower leg and narrowly missed falling as he was pulled inside.

Their young leader crouched on the upper trail, still unable to see the attackers behind their spur of rock. Another arrow was launched at those on the narrow trail to the alcove. This shot skittered harmlessly off the rock wall and the second of the packers was now safe inside the barrier. Yet another shot came, but only stuck in the pack of venison before the third and last load of meat was inside and secure. Still there was the wood hauler, trapped in the middle of the most dangerous portion of the trail. The rest of the foragers held back, temporarily hidden in the shadows of an overhang. Despite the slightly wider ledge there, they too, had little room to maneuver and were forced to hunker down, taking what shelter they could behind their unwieldy packs.

The boy had taken this trail to work in the fields each day, and was aware of a narrow fissure—one splitting the cliff just below the trail. He had often wondered how hard it would be to access the lower portion of the trail in this way, possibly even reach that section lying behind the attackers. It would be a dangerous thing to attempt under the best of conditions, but now, with snow and ice and in poor light, it seemed impossible. Even if he could work his way down quietly enough to remain undetected, he still was uncertain what he might do against so deadly a force. The boy knew in his heart there was no other way. He could only make his way back to the cleft hoping memory had served him correctly and this way down would provide a solution.

As the boy peered into the crevice he was glad there was not light enough to see what he was getting into. Securing his bow and quiver to his back, he eased himself down into the opening using his outstretched arms and feet to bridge the gap between the ragged walls. In only minutes there would be enough light to make the work easier…but that would make him a target as well. He had worked his way down only a few yards when a misjudged foothold caused him to slip and lose his icy hold. For a moment he thought he was finished. Only by jamming one arm and shoulder into the narrowest part of the crack could he keep from sliding into oblivion. It took almost a full minute to recover his courage, reset his foot and continue feeling his way down the fissure. Only a little farther and he should be in position to make the short leap back to the lower trail. One slip, or the dislodging of a single stone could spell death at this point, and only the knowledge that going back was impossible drove him on.

The last few yards were easier than expected and the ledge, when it appeared, more generous than remembered. The pale gray light of dawn was beginning to suffuse the nether reaches of the canyon, and while he could not yet see the enemy, he thought he could feel their presence—occasionally thinking he could detect the scent of them. That might only have been his imagination, but the breeze *was* in his favor, and that alone lent credence to the thought. If the raiders were still where he'd marked them he should now be almost directly above. It was then the boy noticed a large piece of sandstone, sitting almost balanced on the edge of the precipice. It occurred to him, that should he put his back against the wall and push with his feet, he might dislodge the stone and send it over the brink. The question was, would it come crashing down on his enemies, or if he misjudged, fall harmlessly to one side. Either way, his men would be no worse off, and with a little luck just the distraction might allow the trapped wood hauler to retreat to safety. Then too, should the rock-fall cause the raiders to move even a short distance in either direction there was the chance one or more might come into view and provide a target.

When the great stone finally gave way and fell, one of the raiders was actually struck by the rock. The man had moved forward to attempt another shot at the trapped wood-hauler when he was wiped off the face of the cliff. The ensuing rockslide caused the remainder of the raiders to retreat in fear...and as they did, the boy was ready. The first raider to fall went to his knees with an arrow in his back and he rolled off the ledge. The next, hit in the side, tried to turn and go back but his companions panic carried them forward and another was struck, but this time by an arrow from one of the wood-haulers shooting from above.

As they pushed and shoved to escape, the retreating enemy came into full view of those still on the trail above making them easy targets. Before the raiders were out of range several more were hit and mortally wounded. Only one of the wolves had the presence of mind to turn and shoot back. He was lucky and killed a wood-hauler before taking an arrow himself. Probably none of the raiders were left unscathed and the boy doubted those few who made it back to their own country would ever return. In time, there would be others, but for now the villagers knew they had chosen a good place to settle and had new confidence in their ability to defend it. Should they have a wet spring they would prosper in this canyon and the stories passed down would tell of this day and the hard won victory over these…wolves of winter.

14

Provenance

Charlie Yazzie sat reviewing the latest report from the FBI. The investigation into the death of James Erdric had taken a turn, one that warranted further study. The Legal Services Investigator held to his task but was well aware he was being watched.

Harley Ponyboy and Thomas Begay stood at the front desk waiting for some sign they could come on back. The receptionist tried engaging Harley in the sort of light conversation they enjoyed on his previous visit, but he only answered in one or two syllables and kept his main attention on the glass door of Charlie's office. The pair had something of a bone to pick with the Tribal investigator and were growing impatient.

Thomas muttered, "We'll give him another couple of minutes and then we're going on back. There's no sense in keeping us waiting like this."

Harley nodded. "It's probably something pretty important—but I don't see no reason we should have ta stand out here when we could be sitting there in his office more comfy and all."

"Harley, its more than just being 'comfy,' it's a matter of trust. We're his best friends and treating us like we're common walk-in strangers is just not right."

The receptionist, glancing at Harley from time to time, was trying to figure out why he wasn't hitting on her like before. She was thinking she might initiate a little something herself when the buzzer told her it was too late. She frowned. "You boys can go on back… Investigator Yazzie will see you now."

"About time," Thomas muttered, but touched the brim of his hat to the girl. Harley also smiled, and tipped his hat. Time listening to Thomas's whining might have been better spent chatting this girl up. Obviously she was interested, and that was rare these days.

Charlie Yazzie didn't look up when the two came in and continued reading his document— indicating chairs with a wave of his hand. His visitors, frowning, stared across the desk then made little faces at one another.

Thomas coughed finally, and winking at Harley Ponyboy observed, "That must be some pretty interesting reading he's got there."

"Yep," Harley agreed, "Maybe he inherited some money from someone…ta hold his attention like that." Both men chuckled and Thomas took a swipe at Harley with his hat.

Charlie, exasperated, finally looked up then he, too, frowned, pinched the bridge of his nose and studied the pair. "All dressed up I see, new hats and all…must be new hat season on the rez." He almost smiled, "Paul T'Sosi has one, too." He settled back in his chair and raised his eyebrows at them. "Some-one must have gotten paid today." Charlie turned serious when he lay his papers down, "Is the profes-sor all through out at the dig?"

"No, he's still out there piddling around...said there were a few things still needed documenting." Thomas paused and rolled a word around in his head. "Provenance...he said something about 'provenance'." He grinned at Harley. "He paid us off though, most of it anyway, and told us we could take the weekend off and report back on Monday. We still have to help clean up out there, backfill the *kiva* and such."

Harley, ever inquisitive, pointed at the papers on Charlie's desk, and though they were clearly stamped "Confidential" in large red overlay, pursed his lips and asked. "Confidential, huh? What's that all about?"

"They're from the FBI Harley. 'Confidential' means I can't tell anyone what they're about."

"Oh, I know that, but just between us, what are they about?" He canted his head to one side, smiled and murmured, "Have the Feds got something new in the murders?"

Charlie sighed, pushed the papers into the top drawer, and gave Harley a look. "They're confiden-tial Harley. That's about all I can tell you."

The little man puffed up. "Well, what about all the stuff I've told you...about Luanne and all? What about that, huh? That was supposed to be confidential, too."

Charlie leaned across the desk. "You didn't tell me about Luanne...Paul T'Sosi did. You *could* have told me about Luanne, but you didn't, because you thought it was 'confidential.' Now isn't that right?"

Harley squirmed in his chair and looked sideways at Thomas for support.

Thomas shrugged and looked out the window.

Harley frowned and pulled his hat down on his ears. "Well maybe we just better talk about what we came for then." And again looked to his companion to carry the conversation.

Now it was Thomas's turn to be uncomfortable. "Uh... Charlie, we kinda' noticed there *seems* to be something going on with you and Sue. We sorta wondered if it might be us...maybe we're hanging around too much out there lately, or something like that? If that's what it is, we want you to tell us straight up. We don't mean to be a burden on your relationship."

Charlie pushed back in his chair as though distancing himself from the two. They had him. It crossed his mind to just agree and let them think this thing between him and Sue was their fault, but he didn't. And when he did speak, it was in a voice so low they could hardly hear the words. "It's not about you boys...in fact, I don't know what it's about. Sue hasn't been herself lately, moody, and doesn't say much. And when she does talk it's usually about something she thinks I'm doing wrong, or could do better." Charlie stood up, stretched, and walked to the window. Hands clasped behind his back he whispered almost to himself, "Something's bothering her that's for sure."

Harley put on his innocent face and looked up to the ceiling, "She don't have a boyfriend, does she, Charlie?"

Thomas turned a flinty eye on his friend. "Of course she doesn't have a boyfriend Harley...you knothead." He hadn't even considered the possibility of such a thing and after a moment's thought, smiled up at the investigator, "Naa, we'd already heard about it if she had a boyfriend; that kind of news travels fast on the *Dinétah*."

Charlie Yazzie shook his head at the two. "It's nothing like that. It's something else, like she's worried about something...I don't know what it is." He knew his friends were concerned and only trying to help, but it irritated him to have it out in the open like this. That meant he could no longer ignore it, which he now realized was exactly what he had been doing. When he turned from the window he said, "I guess I better have a talk with her tonight and see if we can't work it out...whatever it is...before the neighbors start asking questions." He meant this last part as a joke but saw the two look at one another as though that might already be the case.

After Harley Ponyboy and Thomas Begay left the office, Charlie sat back and took a good hard look at himself. He wasn't at all sure he liked what he saw. Maybe this wasn't just about Sue after all.

~~~~~~

George Custer thought it a sad thing that so interesting a site should be left for another time, but he felt the recent murders, and their ties to the project, made it dangerous to continue. He himself was now wearing a sidearm at all times and even Thomas Begay was talking about buying a gun.

George planned only to locate, and record, any suspected burials against the back wall of the alcove. It was a favorite place for the Anasazi to bury their dead—possibly because the digging was easy and close by. They seemed to like having their dead near them. Aside from the far end of the alcove, where signs of a spring or at least a seep of some sort were still apparent, the base of the back wall was dust dry, with bedrock only a couple of feet down. A nice protected place to put the dead despite having turkey pens on top of them. The professor considered the recording of these burial sites an integral part of his documentation, and his job. He was well aware that not everyone in the business thought it necessary, but for him it was.

The professor could see now that Paul T'Sosi on his previous visit had already located one of the burials and had it nearly uncovered. The old singer had a natural sense of these things, despite, or perhaps because of, a natural aversion to the dead. He hadn't mentioned his work along the wall. Paul had grown more forgetful these last months and the professor found himself rechecking a good many of the old man's assigned tasks. He wouldn't have minded so much in more ordinary times, but this particular project left him little time to follow up on the work of others.

As part of his decision to mothball the entire site George was about to fill in the shallow excavation when he noticed just a tiny corner of textile or some sort of woven material.

The professor's curiosity kicked in and he couldn't resist taking a closer look. He had not yet turned in the accumulated collection of specimens from the project. Other than the mummified remains of the girl they had come to call the "Swallow Keep-er." He thought there was probably little of professional interest, either scientifically or for display. Most museums' backrooms were already filled with similar artifacts to the point of becoming a burden on strained institutional budgets. Many curators had a hard time even keeping up with the cataloging of what they already had stored. The professor had no doubt there were still plenty of similar specimens left to find, should one know where to look. All this aside he could not help but take another shovel-full…then another…then the trowel and finally the whiskbroom. Soon he was looking at what appeared to be a hurried interment. It was a choice spot so most likely from early on in the settlement's history.

Funerary offerings included a rather plain look-ing bowl along with a simple, undecorated mug, but there was also a nicely made bow and handful of ar-rows. The professor grew more pensive as he regarded these things, and used extra care in remov-ing the roughly woven layer of matting covering the remains. He was then looking at what appeared to be a mature male, not mummified, but with skeletal re-mains in good condition. It was only as he examined the burial more closely that he noticed first one, then a second arrowhead; one just inside the rib cage, and yet another embedded in the tibia of the lower left leg.

It was now obvious what had brought the person to so unhappy an end. But more important to the professor was that the man had clearly suffered these mortal wounds in some sort of conflict, more than likely close by. That would mean a confrontation near, or in the village itself. The body would not have been retrieved from any great distance. The professor surmised this village had come under attack at some point, but it would seem their enemies had been driven off as his previous observations indicated the little settlement remained occupied by these people for many years following this period. This particular burial was covered with what appeared to be turkey droppings, in what must have been a pen of some sort.

George Custer stood finally, and rubbed his lower back, thinking to himself he should retrieve his water bottle left in another part of the ruin, but as he walked to the edge of the alcove he could see someone coming up the trail from the road. He had become so engrossed in the burial he'd not heard the vehicle. As the man drew closer the professor still did not recognize him and again cursed the ancient rock slide that made the site so accessible. The man appeared to be close to his own age, plainly dressed, and of a determined nature. When he looked up and saw he was being watched the man put on a smile and raised a hand in greeting. The professor knew almost immediately then who it was—he was not likely to forget that cold and cynical smile.

William Crawley was breathing hard as he climbed the remaining pile of rubble and then stood a moment surveying the site. "Found anything good, have you?" he asked, holding out a hand, "How have you been, George?" Not waiting for an answer he cocked his head to one side, "It's been a while hasn't it?

George Custer hesitated a moment before taking the hand, but didn't bother to return the smile when he answered, "Hello Bill...back in the states I see. I believe you were in Guatemala last I heard. How was it down there?" The professor knew exactly how it had been for Crawley in Guatemala but wondered what spin the man would put on the goings on whispered among the fraternity.

"Oh, you know, those digs down there are all pretty much the same George, you've been there yourself from what I recall." The archaeologist seemed ambivalent enough toward the obviously loaded question but it set the tone for the conversation and both men were now on their guard.

Crawley pointed to the new revolver on the professor's hip. "I see you're 'packing' George. Rattlesnakes?"

I suppose you could say that. I'm sure you've heard about the looting in the area. One can't be too careful when that sort of people are about." He eyed his former colleague up and down. "I've never really minded a rattlesnake, Bill, as long as he rattles now and again...it's those quiet ones that will get you." This was one of the professor's favorite old sayings and he thought it never more appropriate than now.

Crawley laughed, grudgingly nodded agreement, and then looked out across the ruin to a shovel handle sticking up above a mound of dirt. "Is that a burial along that back wall George? Looks like a clever person might uncover a mummy or two in these conditions...dry as it is and all."

"You'd think so, wouldn't you, but no, that's not the case this time." The professor didn't elaborate or even look back toward the burial in question, only grimaced and with a glint in his eye questioned his old colleague further. "I hear you're working up this way again? 'Contract work,' as I understand it? That right?"

Crawley didn't hesitate or bother to make excuses when he answered, "In a manner of speaking, I guess that's about right. 'Salvage work' actually! We may as well call it what it is George. I know 'Contract Archaeology' seems to be the term bandied about these days, but that has always struck me as...somehow pretentious. I'm actually more in the business of placing quality artifacts in the hands of interested collectors—universities and museums for the most part, but a few private collectors, too, should the paperwork be right, and of course the price—It's always about price in the end, isn't it, George?"

The professor said nothing but moved slightly to block the other's view of the burial though he doubted much could be seen from this distance. "Plan on being around this part of the country much longer, do you, Bill?" Dr. Custer narrowed his eyes when he continued, "Any 'contracts' in the works now?" The professor was suspicious of William Crawley's motives in arriving unexpected like this. In truth, he would have thought the man should be embarrassed to show his face among legitimate academics. It occurred to him his visitor had been waiting until George was alone before dropping by. It was almost all the professor could do then to keep his hand from straying near his revolver. Crawley wasn't armed as far as he could see and it seemed silly to suspect the portly, balding little man of any sort of violence, but his reputation *had* preceded him and it was one filled with the innuendo of many dark deeds.

As though reading Custer's mind, Crawley looked away for a moment. "I've heard you've uncovered a rather unusual piece here, George; a turquoise amulet or fetish, and was wondering if I might have a look at it?" The man held up a cautionary finger, "No more than academic curiosity, I can assure you." Seeing little positive response, Crawley's next statement was more pointed. "I would consider it a professional courtesy George."

"Yes, well, unfortunately that piece is in the hands of the FBI at the moment and it may be a while before it's available." George Armstrong Custer fixed the other archaeologist with a flinty gaze. "As you might also have heard, the amulet has been linked to the murder of one, and quite possibly two men, as far as I know."

"Well, I'm sorry to hear that, George. News of the murders is all over the media, but I had no idea the amulet was involved." He smiled. "Should you come back into possession of it you might want to give me a call." He passed the professor his card. "You might find it interesting to learn how much these things are worth these days... just between you and me, of course."

Up to this point Dr. Custer had attempted to conceal his full disdain for the man but it was apparent when he answered, "I don't think so Bill. You know me, I don't deal in artifacts, nor do I intend to in the future, no matter what the price."

"Never say never, George. Fortunes change, and it is fortunes that are being made in the gray market right now. With the proper provenance attached, the trade can be...how shall I put this? Quite safe, legally speaking." With this William Crawley turned on his heel and purposefully strode back the way he had come, working his way through the slide rock, and on down to the road.

There was that word again, "Provenance." It had become a catchphrase in the parlance of those involved in the acquisition of antiquities, legal or otherwise. Proper documentation was the key to providing or denying legal distribution of artifacts. Provenance? It was always the first question out of buyers' mouths.

George Custer watched as the once-respected academic got in his car and without even a glance in his rear view mirror, started back the way he had come. The man had been well thought of in their early days at UNM. Many felt he would go far given his natural talent and clear dedication to the science. How he had come to such a sorry pass was still the focus of many a conversation among his fellows at the university. *Who can say what devils drive such a man.* The visit reminded the professor he should be checking with Agent Mayfield as to the status of the amulet. Charlie Yazzie was of the opinion that photo documentation alone should suffice in any sort of courtroom proceeding. It would be unusual, he thought, to require so rare a piece be retained as physical evidence. It was, after all, not a smoking gun.

As it grew dark Professor Custer couldn't shake the feeling he was being watched, and became uncomfortable at the thought of it. Harley Ponyboy and Thomas Begay would be back in another day and then he thought the three of them could wrap things up pretty quickly. He looked forward to taking a few days off, perhaps running up to Cortez for a little visit with Aida Winters. They still were corresponding on a sporadic basis and he tried to drop by every month or so. Occasionally they drove into Cortez for dinner, but that was about as far as it went these days. He was afraid that fire might finally be dying out—at least for one of them. In any case it wouldn't hurt to give it a last go. He thought he might make one last attempt at reconciliation. Aida had only Thomas Begay's children to focus on…and he had no one at all. They were both getting on and he doubted either would have many more opportunities down the road.

That night in his tent Professor Custer read later than he intended, not turning out the light until nearly midnight. Only a short time after that, as he was drifting off, he thought he heard the faraway sound of a car, or truck perhaps, but couldn't be certain and fell asleep thinking he should get up and check it out…but he didn't.

15

Friends

Thomas Begay had thought himself nearly immune to his wife's insistent badgering about the two murder investigations. Due to his friendship with Tribal Investigator Charlie Yazzie, she had somehow perceived the idea he was privy to secret information. He tried to explain that the FBI had let it be known they would no longer tolerate information being passed among the various tribal agencies. They felt local authorities were prone to mishandle confidential information…and that was probably true. Navajo law enforcement probably was a little lax in that regard, but only in their effort to compare notes and quantify how little had been sent them. They resented the FBI's notoriously superficial reports, filled with double-speak, and oftentimes incomplete when it came to the real goods.

Nonetheless, Lucy Tallwoman was not one to be denied and secretly vowed to stick with her friend Sue Yazzie, who was equally displeased with her husband's tight-lipped refusal to share. Only the day before Sue told Lucy she was tired of relying on the radio for the "latest" news in the murders when her own husband was obviously better informed. Then too, there was that other thing only the two of them knew. Lucy was not sure why her friend was so adamant no one else should know just yet, but for now she would keep the secret.

Thomas Begay looked at the plate his wife brought him and knew instantly it was retaliation for his refusal to "spill the beans," as she put it. It was mutton, but a poor cut and overcooked. He said nothing, pretended to enjoy it, and knew anything else might lead to even stricter measures. His father-in-law had eaten early and was already asleep in the old hogan behind the house. He doubted the old man had been served this same dish. Paul T'Sosi wouldn't have stood for it. He sensed there was more to this than he knew, and wondered if he should bring it up with the old singer in the morning.

~~~~~~

When Thomas picked up Harley Ponyboy for the trip back up to the dig, his friend saw immediately he was out of sorts yet hesitated to ask why. Thomas Begay tended to be a little testy when it came to personal matters.

After a few miles of total silence Harley could see Thomas's mood had not improved and figured it time to get things out in the open, though as gently as possible. "So what's with the frogmouth this morning Big Boy?"

Thomas half-turned and glared at the little man. "What the hell are you talking about, Shorty"?

When Thomas called him Shorty, Harley knew there was no point in pursuing it further, and turned to the window with a frown. Now they both had frogmouths and it was a long ride to the dig.

Professor Custer heard Thomas's diesel truck coming for quite some distance and automatically added to the pancake batter and threw extra slices of bacon in the pan. He knew the two liked pancakes and bacon and would be pleased he'd thought of them.

Harley was the first one through the tent flap and smiled as he sniffed and guessed breakfast was near ready. "That smells good George." then indicated a still stoic Thomas with a thumb over his shoulder. "Doc, don't pay no attention to 'String Bean' here. His nose is out of joint this morning, so he probably can't smell those pancakes."

The professor glanced at Thomas and chuckled, then saw immediately it was the wrong thing to do, and turned grimly to the bacon sputtering in the pan; now it was three frogmouths for breakfast. George carried a huge plate of pancakes to the table then went back for the bacon and coffee pot. He'd already set the table with plates and cups when he heard the truck coming.

"Were either of you two aware Paul T'Sosi had been digging into a burial at the back wall of the alcove?" The professor was sure one of the two would have noticed the old man digging around back there.

Harley looked up, mouth full of pancakes, but didn't let that stop him from answering though it did make him a bit hard to understand. "I saw him back there, but he never said anything about a burial." He turned to Thomas. "Did the old man say anything to you about a burial?"

Thomas, who had spent more time at boarding school than Harley, finished swallowing his mouthful before his terse reply. "No, he didn't."

"Well," the professor said, "He did, and it's turned out to be an unusual one too—male about twenty years old, with two arrowheads in him. Looks to me like these people might have come under siege at some point."

Harley looked up from his plate, obviously interested. "Maybe it was just a jealous husband from right here in the village?" and then chortled over his little joke

"No, they weren't Anasazi arrow points, they're rougher and not so finely knapped." The archaeologist was adamant. "It was outsiders, no doubt about it. The question is, where did they come from and who were they?" The professor peered in the direction of the burial as though he could see through the canvas wall. "It's an awfully shallow interment. I'm not so sure this one should be left in place."

"*In situ* you mean?" Since Harley had learned the meaning of the phrase he used it whenever possible, especially in Thomas's presence.

Thomas rolled his eyes, and swallowing the last of his coffee, appeared to take a turn for the better as he asked what else had happened in their days off.

George Custer considered the two *Diné* for a moment, wondering if he should tell them about the visit from William Crawley but decided there was no reason not to. It might put them on their guard to be aware of the man and what he was capable of.

As the professor told them about their business competitor's visit, Thomas, still mopping up his pancakes, raised his head and ventured the opinion, "I don't think we should leave anyone alone in camp for a while, at least not at night."

It was then Harley mentioned spotting unfamiliar tire tracks when they parked Thomas's diesel earlier. Harley made a habit of taking notice of such things thinking it sharpened his skills as a tracker. "They were big tires... truck tires and fairly new."

"It could be this Crawley fellow came back in the night." Thomas offered.

The professor thought about this before saying, "Could be, but he was driving a regular car when he was here yesterday and not a truck."

Harley nodded at this then changed the subject, bringing up the fact that he felt better with the professor having the gun. He looked over at Thomas and asked George if he might give them a little demonstration of his skill with the weapon. He was prone to stick up for the doctor and only the day before had taken exception to Thomas Begay doubting the professor's ability with the revolver.

The professor hemmed and hawed as he often did when uncertain, and in the end, said he probably was not quite as proficient as he once had been...but that he would be happy to engage in a little target practice with them. He had brought along plenty of ammunition and suggested they all take a turn with the weapon, then unexpectedly declared whoever proved to be the best shot could be in charge of security and allowed to pack the big revolver around. The gun had become a constant hindrance to his work, he said, if one of them proved to be a better shot he would be happy to relinquish it. Thomas perked up considerably at this development and grinned then winked at Harley.

The three of them walked a short distance from camp, and brought a small sack of empty tin cans along with them; Harley set these up on a small log a reasonable distance away. The professor brought out the ammunition, passed out a handful of cartridges to each one smiling when he cautioned, "This gun might be of a larger caliber than you boys are used to."

Harley Ponyboy had only limited experience with handguns in general and particularly not with a .357 whose kick and the loud report surprised him. He hit none of the five cans, though one was knocked over by a bullet whizzing past it. He looked a little crestfallen as he passed the revolver to Thomas, who smiled to himself as he hefted the gun a few times to get the feel of it, then reloaded and took a shooter's stance, gripping the gun with both hands, as he had seen his nephew Billy Red Clay do when demonstrating his police training.

Thomas's first shot hit the log just below one of the five cans. Harley smiled and said he'd done good...if that was the actual can he had been aiming at. Thomas frowned, examined the sights, then fired another round, which went a tad high and only clipped a short twig off a bush behind the log. He now appeared a little nervous, but on his next shot hit a can just at the lower rim, which sent it spinning into the next one, and knocking both cans off the log. Thomas immediately called it two hits.

Harley began to protest but the professor held up a hand, saying, "No, Harley, that's all right, we'll let it stand; two it is."

Thomas, grinning now, took careful aim and touched off a final round, which clearly went wide, leaving the remaining cans unscathed. He again frowned and pretended to check the sights before handing the weapon back to the professor. "I'd get those sights checked Doc."

Custer acknowledged this with a grunt and made a point of saying, "For not having shot a gun like this before, that's actually pretty good shooting, boys. A little more practice should bring you right along."

As the professor reloaded, Harley set the cans back up on the log. When he returned George nodded, then threw the gun up and hit four of the five cans in quick succession. On the last shot the handgun only clicked and the professor said, "Oops! I guess I only put in four rounds." Then he smiled. "I probably wouldn't have hit that last can anyway."

Thomas looked at Harley who was grinning ear to ear, and wondered if his friend had known how well the professor could shoot. "Where'd you learn to shoot like that Doc?"

"Oh, shooters go back a long way among my people, I still have family in Northern Ireland who keep British Webleys wrapped in oilcloth and buried in their back yards...just in case." He was grinning as he said this and its full political significance winged past the two Navajo. Still they were impressed.

The professor slipped the revolver back in its holster. "Well, boys, it looks like site security will remain under my jurisdiction for a while yet. I hope everyone feels safer now." He then turned and walked nonchalantly back to camp but when he was out of earshot couldn't help chuckling to himself.

While Harley and Thomas began gathering gear and packing up specimens, George Custer thought he'd better check things out at the dig. Only moments later he came hurrying back with a concerned look on his face.

Harley stopped wrapping newspaper around a corrugated cooking pot and raised his eyebrows at the professor. "Forget something, George?"

"Yes, I forgot to check on that truck I heard last night. Apparently we had another visitor up at the dig." The grim faced professor surveyed the camp. "Funny, the only thing I can find out of place up there is the new burial by the back wall."

Thomas walked up about that time ready to carry another load down to the truck. He'd heard a little of the conversation and asked, "Someone messing with that burial?"

"Not exactly, but I think someone did leave us a message...or more likely a warning. The hands are now crossed over its chest.

After a short reflection Thomas decided it might just be local kids. "They are all over this country at night, drinking and carrying on like wild Indians. They make all sorts of mischief in these old ruins; they're not afraid of them like the old people."

The professor wasn't so sure. "I somehow doubt this was kids. It took someone with a pretty good knowledge of human anatomy to place those bones so precisely. I think someone wants us to know they're watching, though to what end I can't imagine." George paused, seeming undecided what to do, but then said, "I think I'd better run into town and have a little talk with Charlie Yazzie."

Harley put down the half-wrapped pot. "I'll go up to the dig and take a look around, too, Doc.—if it was kids there should be some sign of them." When he'd thought about it a moment he added, "I'll go back down to the road, too, and take a better look at those tire tracks. There's something a little weird about all this."

Thomas spoke up, "If it's not kids it might well be some sort of witchery, at least that's how it seems to me." He aimed this last at Harley and was pleased to see him miss a step and curse.

George Custer shook his head and thought, *this is all we need! They'll probably insist on another ceremony if Harley can't come up with a better explanation.*

~~~~~~~

Charlie Yazzie noticed the message from Billy Red Clay as soon as he entered the office. He knew Billy was working on the Karl Hoffman shooting in his spare time, anxious to clear his name in the investigation, despite being warned anything he turned up might be considered inadmissible in a court of law. Billy's note asked if they could meet for coffee at the Diné Bikeyah. Charlie didn't like the idea of going behind Captain Beyale's back and was well aware the

FBI would like it even less. Still, he owed Billy a favor or two and didn't see how having a coffee with the Tribal officer would be a problem.

The restaurant was quiet. The mid-morning rush had subsided, and there were only a few older locals scattered around the room. Charlie chose his usual booth near the back and ordered a cinnamon roll with his coffee. He was a few minutes early and fell into quiet introspection as he waited for his order. How many times had he and Sue sat at this same booth and had coffee or lunch—back when she was still Sue Hanagarni working for Legal Services. It seemed like a long time ago, but then three years was a long time, and it was flying by since the birth of their son. Joseph Wiley would be four before they knew it and ready for preschool. Sue mentioned several times she thought she might return to work when the boy started school. She had worked her way up to office manager before leaving Legal Services to have the baby. Sue was still considered the best manager they'd ever had. While the current crop of office help left a lot to be desired, he still wasn't sure he would be comfortable with her coming back, not to mention, administration had changed. Much stricter rules applied regarding nepotism. The reservation was still the reservation; it seemed like everyone was related one way or another. He still hadn't managed to have that little talk with her though he'd been prepping for it. The truth was he was afraid it wasn't going to be a "little" talk at all. He wasn't sure he was ready.

Billy Red Clay paused at the door and looked toward the back booth. Charlie Yazzie appeared lost in thought and hadn't noticed him. Billy gave a little half-wave in that direction as he started back and was nearly there when he heard a voice behind him. It was Professor Custer. "Glad I caught you, the receptionist said I'd find you and Charlie here." They were at the booth now. Charlie Yazzie blinked at the two of them and, for a split second, appeared surprised. He extended a hand to the tribal officer and then to George Custer who appeared a little hesitant and unsure.

"Looked like you were having some deep thinking going on." Billy shook hands with the investigator.

"Yes, I was," Charlie admitted and smiled at the pair.

The professor slid in beside him then looked over at Billy Red Clay, "I hope I'm not interrupting a private meeting?"

"Not really, there were just a few things I needed to talk over with Charlie, and actually, I had a question or two you might be able to help with."

Charlie looked puzzled, "Sounds like you two might be on the same track this morning." The waitress came and took the latecomers' order, then smiled at Charlie, "How's that cinnamon roll?"

Charlie assured her it was good as usual, and couldn't help but notice the warm smile but hoped it wasn't due to any perceived notion he and Sue weren't getting along. The girls at the *Diné Bikeyah* were long time admirers of Charlie Yazzie, and this one had seemed particularly disappointed when he married Sue. He was becoming paranoid since his talk with Thomas and Harley, and was nearly convinced someone was spreading rumors. Charlie turned to the professor. "What's on your mind George?" He decided he would address the professor first, in case Billy Red Clay had something more private to discuss later.

The professor brought the two up to speed on what happened out at the dig, including the visit from William Crawley. He wanted that conversation to be on record. There was also the matter of the midnight visit to the alcove the night before. Custer laid all this out for the two and immediately felt better having it reported to the proper authorities, albeit unofficially.

"Hmm," Billy Red Clay said, as though reading the professor's mind, "I'll file a report on the desecration of the grave when I get back to the office. Actually, some of this ties into what I wanted to talk to Charlie about." He turned to the investigator who had a mouthful of cinnamon roll. "When you were out at Luanne Keyonie's place, did you by chance talk to her mother, Martha? There are rumblings she might be on the Hopi tribal board soon. Her feelings against excavating those ruins are pretty strong according to some people I've talked to."

Charlie shook his head. "No, she wasn't home at the time but her daughter mentioned she wasn't very happy about the work up at the site."

The professor took a quick drink of coffee, nearly burned his mouth, and frowned at the cup before protesting. "Surely you boys don't think she was the one who was up at the alcove last night."

Billy looked at the professor, "Here's something you may not know. Martha works as a nurse and physician's assistant at the clinic in Shiprock, and after hearing your account of the placement of skeletal parts up at the dig, it reminded me how serious she is in taking a stand against those excavations up there. She is a staunch Indian Rights advocate, and certainly has the expertise to reposition those bones. Just a thought of course, but maybe worth looking into."

The professor held up a hand, "Well, some of the bones did still have connective tissue holding them together, at least somewhat, but they were rearranged by someone who obviously had some training." He snorted, "But it could have been William Crawley, too. He would be my first choice. The man has the knowhow, and would have the most to gain if my outfit was out of the way." He looked thoughtfully up at the ceiling, "He's been known to intimidate rivals before...and worse. If the stories out of Central America are true."

Billy Red Clay spoke again, "Tribal police now have several suspects on their list in the Karl Hoffman murder, including me of course," The young officer frowned at the thought of it but went on, "James Erdric is still suspect, too, no one can corroborate his statement that he was there with the road crew at the time of the shooting." Billy held up his hands, "Now, that he's dead no one can seem to remember *where* the man was when Hoffman was shot. The wild card is this William Crawley. There's no doubt he had business dealings with both Hoffman and Erdric, but with both of them dead, it's unclear exactly what that business was.

The Navajo policeman continued, "The FBI, of course, zeroed in on Jimmy John in Erdric's murder from the first, and would like to tie him to the Hoffman killing, too. That would make a nice little package." He shook his head, "They're saying they're close to an announcement in the cases. But no one at Tribal has a clue as to what that announcement might be. Their reports have trailed off to nothing lately. It's getting a little frustrating."

Charlie had been taking all this in, but the only new information he'd heard was concerning Martha Keyoni. He thought her involvement would be a stretch by any reasonable measure. They were missing something important somewhere, and he had the odd feeling he was the one who dropped the ball; upon reflection, he thought he knew where he dropped it.

~~~~~~

Sue Hanagarni-Begay was a woman of action, as was Lucy Tallwoman. When they met in Farmington for some shopping and a quick breakfast at McDonalds, it was to let the kids play in the children's section, while they talked about the murders they thought were affecting the *hozo* of so many. They were thinking people seemed more wary, and even those who'd known each other for years were now suspicious of one another. Many felt the mysterious death of Danny Hat was surrounded with an aura of witchcraft, an idea that was spreading.

Luanne Keyoni had been to see Paul T'Sosi several times in the last week, but neither she, nor Paul would say why. The woman did, however, manage to corner Lucy each visit, in regard to what she might have learned from Thomas or Harley.

When Lucy got around to asking Sue if she'd told Charlie her secret, she studied her friend's face and was struck by the total lack of emotion. "I think it's time you told him you're pregnant. I know there were a lot of problems with Joseph Wiley, but this time will be different—you'll see." She looked over at her stepchildren. Ida Marie was at the top of the slide and waving. She smiled and waved back at the girl, then became serious again. "You are going to start showing soon anyway. Better to tell him now and get it over with."

"Really? Will it be different next time? That doctor said the same thing that happened with Joseph Wiley could happen again. I know you think it was a curse that caused it all. But even back then, Charlie said he didn't think it was safe to have another child——curse or no curse. I think he's still afraid something could go wrong." She paused, "Too late now though." Then followed her friend's gaze and watched as Joseph Wiley laughed as Caleb Begay held him up for their inspection; the front of his pants was wet.

~~~~~~

Thomas Begay and Harley Ponyboy had hardly finished washing the breakfast dishes when there came a faint shout from the parking area. The men looked at one another and both frowned. Thomas dried his hands on a towel and moved toward the door. Harley turned and followed, wiping his hands on his pants as he came. Thomas shaded his eyes against the morning sun but waited for his friend to make any final assessment. Harley stared down at the pickup truck for only a moment before murmuring, "looks like a woman ta me...by herself, too." He threw up his hands, "Oh, hell, it's Martha Keyoni, now what?" He didn't know if he was up to a round with Luanne's mother.

Thomas normally would have taken charge at this point, but deferred to Harley due to his ties with the Keyoni family. "Do you think we should go down there...at least keep her away from the site? That burial is still open you know."

"Naa, let her come up here if she wants ta talk ta someone so bad." Harley hoped she would just go away, but knew that wasn't likely. He'd known Martha since he was little; she wasn't one to back down. He had never liked the woman, even as a child. She always seemed a little mean natured in his view. She even tried to turn Luanne against him when she thought they were becoming romantically inclined. After thinking about the open burial for a moment he said, "Crap!" and started down through the rubble, Thomas, grinning now, was right behind him.

"Harley Ponyboy, you sonofabitch!" Martha yelled as they drew nearer, "What do you think you're doing to my people up there?"

They were closer now and Harley's face was grim as he narrowed his eyes at the woman and held up a hand. "Now Martha, you know we have a right ta be here—we're only doin' our job. The professor ain't here right now. If you got questions you better come back later and talk to him." He could hear Thomas chuckling behind him but still was glad to have the backup. He knew Thomas would explain it to her in more serious terms if she didn't go away. He hoped it wouldn't come to that. There was still a possibility he and Luanne might someday get together after all this was over, though he could see the chances of that growing slimmer by the minute.

Martha Keyoni glared at them both, and edged a few steps closer. Thomas Begay stepped in front of Harley then and put both hands out in front of him. "Mrs. Keyoni," he said gently, "I understand you are upset right now...but I think it would be best to do what Harley says and come back when the professor is here," Thomas advanced a step further, "Otherwise I may have to do something that will put us both in jail." He said all this quite calmly while looking the woman directly in the eye, a thing he preferred not to do. Something in Thomas's manner alerted the woman to some hidden sense of danger and she hesitated then backed off a step.

"I'll be back!" She said fiercely, and turned to her truck. Martha Keyoni put the truck in gear, and as she glanced back at the two men couldn't help feeling she had just escaped a situation that could have turned out much worse.

Thomas Begay had never assaulted a woman in his life, but then Martha Keyoni had no way of knowing that.

After Martha was well up the road Harley walked over to where her truck was parked and examined the tire tracks. "This isn't the same truck that was up here in the middle of the night."

16

1075 A.D.

Rain

After their confrontation with the wolves, life in the village gradually settled back into a more familiar pattern. Despite dwindling stores, most thought things were looking up. The elders rationed food but thought there would probably be enough to see them through. As the deer, thin though they were, followed the snow line back up the mesa, hunters managed to bring a few down and that helped.

Spring brought rain in quantities not seen in several years; if it continued it might prove enough to fill the newly repaired dams, and small reservoirs. As the snow went off the mesas work began on the ditches. People made ready to plant, meeting in the *kivas* for ceremonies that gave thanks. Word eventually filtered in from the south that the larger towns had not been so lucky; the rain avoided them and they faced even harsher conditions than the last season.

The boy's sister was now called a seer. She foretold the return of rain and smaller things some people had forgotten; she was held in ever-higher esteem. She and her old father were allotted a more generous share of the remaining food. People brought rabbit fur blankets to keep her warm, and a few supple deer hides for her bed. Still her condition worsened and the boy thought only the healing warmth of the sun could help. He prayed to the Gods she might hold out long enough to take advantage of better weather. His new wife knew something of herbs, how to make potions with healing properties, and she applied this knowledge in an effort to keep the girl going. She went each day to grind their corn and make hot soups and stews that brought some measure of comfort. Still the girl grew weaker, causing her father to worry and work even harder to make his daughter comfortable.

And so it was that winter passed into spring and warmth returned once again to the canyon lands. The few young boys left to the clans scoured the upper canyons for anything edible. They brought home rabbits, ground squirrels, and other small creatures. The orphan girl joined the boys, and it was she that frightened a hen turkey from her nest and discovered a clutch of newly hatched young, caught some, and brought them back to the village. An old man built a pen at the back of the alcove and saw to their care. The liquid chirp of the poults was music to the ears of the old people who knew there would eventually be eggs and feathers to weave into blankets. They smiled upon the girl who brought the birds causing the boys of the village to declare they too would find young turkeys, and they did. It then became the boys' job to find insects and the tender young plants the birds favored. Soon the boys wished they had not found the birds and could again spend their time hunting and exploring the canyons.

The village's remaining female dog delivered pups, only a few, but they were welcome, and would one day make life easier both for the hunters, and for the boys who would later guard the fields.

Finally, the elders were pleased to see several women were with child, including the boy's wife, whose rescue the previous fall was already a fading memory. Things had come full circle and the elders were more satisfied with their decision to leave their old home, certain now it had been the right thing to do. The old town with its hectic life and new ways of thinking, new Gods even, was now only a distant memory. It was rumored things had gone from bad to worse there. The new holy men seemed unable to summon the rain as once they had done and warned there might have to be sacrifices...sacrifices of a sort never dreamed of before.

When the young couple's child was born, it was a boy, and the corn was just peeking from the red dirt of the fields. The corn was a long time coming, planted deep, so its roots would follow the water down. The boy's wife's people, industrious builders and farmers, were prospering; a few had already intermarried with the others, together they had built yet another *kiva*. The little alcove was filling fast. The only direction left was up, but even that space was limited.

It was a warm morning in midsummer when the boy's father died working in the fields. No one could find a reason for it other than his time had come; everyone wondered what would now become of his daughter and her predictions. Many depended on her advice and worried now about the future. They buried the old man close by the ruined houses of those who first farmed those plots, and the boy wondered how he would get along without him.

The care of the boy's sister was taken over by him and his wife, and what with the new baby and work with the crops, their days were long and full. But they were young and strong and didn't mind the work—it was the same for everyone, the only life any of them knew. The boy's sister rallied somewhat as the weather warmed, just as she always did, and the boy hoped the change would be a lasting one, just as he always did. The girl remained alert, her predictions, for the most part, accurate. She continued to guide the elders in ways so subtle they thought the ideas were their own.

Occasionally small band of immigrants from the larger towns far to the south passed through. The old towns had become unbearable they said, with the common people doing more than their share of work and receiving less in return. Some of the travelers even asked if they might stay there and live in the village with them. These people, often from their old town, were told, "No, there is no more room in our village, the fields are unable to support more mouths." Some pilgrims looked resentful, a few became surly, but in the end they moved on to whatever fate awaited them farther east in the hinterlands.

The boy was well aware that even their own time there was limited, and one day they or their children would have to move on and start afresh. It was the way it had always been, the soil would become depleted despite their best farming techniques. The trees would disappear into firewood and building. And the wild game hunted so incessantly as to be killed out, or forced to migrate beyond their grasp. Life was not sustainable in one place, at least not forever. He thought the secret to living in this country was in knowing when to move on.

By late summer the crops were growing well, the beans and squash were in bloom, and there still was a bit of reserve water left in the holding ponds. The people were guarded in their outlook, but many thought the worst might well be over. And for a while at least, the rain continued to work its way up from the south and west, and life was as good as could be expected. Rumors from the far settlements reported the wandering tribes of the north were quiet and not causing concern in the borderlands; some said those people had followed the game to the great middle parks in the mountains—to make meat. Everyone knew that might change very quickly and were ever on their guard.

The boy and his wife often spoke of her cousin, who fought so valiantly to rescue her the previous year. She said it was probably the blood of the holy men from the south that caused him to be so big and so fierce a fighter. Probably, that was what alienated him from the others. In death, he had finally gained acceptance and his name was praised among his people. Except for the girl's mother the couple's parents were dead and buried now, and her mother, too, seemed to be failing. They thought the orphan girl would eventually come to live with them, and help with her husband's sister. She hoped the young girl would eventually learn something from the seer, and possibly even develop a talent for manipulating the elders as the seer herself had done. The girl already had a way with people. That was her true power. She would learn the healing herbs and how to prepare them and understand their uses...that too, would stand her in good stead among the clans. The girl had a future that could not be denied.

~~~~~~

It was climbing on toward fall when the seer died, and she was buried in a manner befitting one of her importance. She had been in remarkably good health that summer and her death came without warning, as though she simply could not bear the burden of another winter. Just before her burial was closed the last woman of the Swallow Clan came forward, took off her turquoise amulet, and laid it on the dead girl's breast, covering it with a shallow bowl from her childhood. *At last,* she thought, *this poor tortured creature will fly with the swallows.*

17

The Predicament

Senior FBI Agent Eldon Mayfield paced back and forth and hadn't said a word in several minutes. *Charlie Yazzie is becoming a pain*, he thought though he was forced to admit the man had his uses. The Legal Services Investigator seemed to have eyes and ears everywhere on the reservation, while he himself seemed unable to forge a connection with these independent minded people. If it weren't for his Liaison Officer Billy Red Clay he wouldn't know what was going on outside his own doors. "So, you say someone's been messing about Professor Custer's site?" He paused thoughtfully for a moment, "And Martha Keyoni threatened his workers?" The FBI man pretended to think about this for a further moment before turning to Charlie Yazzie. "Have you spoken to the woman yourself?"

"No, I haven't, I only know what Harley Ponyboy and Thomas Begay told me...but I imagine it's about right. They did say they expect more interference from her, if not outright violence. She's apparently quite upset. They told her to come back when the professor was there, but she never did."

"Did Thomas Begay threaten her in any way?" Agent Mayfield was familiar with both Thomas and Harley and didn't think the question unreasonable.

Charlie looked unsure, "Not that they mentioned, but I doubt they would have said anything to me if they had threatened her."

"I'm sure they wouldn't," The agent smiled and waved this away, and wearily sat himself down. "What time was this report filed?"

Billy Red Clay thumbed through a folder in his lap, withdrew a complaint form. "The report was filed yesterday afternoon about 1 P.M. according to this. The policeman was following the words with a forefinger. "Martha Keyoni says she was merely expressing her opinion when the two men became abusive, and that was when Thomas Begay threatened her."

"Threatened her with what...?" Charlie didn't doubt for a minute that Thomas might have warned the woman off, but not without provocation.

Billy Red Clay continued running a finger across the page. "She didn't say. Officer Hastiin Sosi took the complaint, and he said she seemed most concerned that they wouldn't comply with her request to shut down." He skipped a few lines. "Unc... uh, Thomas Begay, says they were already in the process of shutting down and that she was the one who became abusive." Billy smiled, "Thomas Begay is not one to take any guff off anyone, but I doubt he intended her any harm. Had she been a man it might have been different of course."

Agent Mayfield pushed back in his chair and sighed. "Gentlemen, your report comes a little late. Field Agent Fred Smith arrested Martha Keyoni this morning at 8:30 A.M. for the murder of Karl Hoffman." The FBI agent was gratified to see the looks of astonishment from the two Navajo, and decided to let this announcement sink in a bit before going on. "Despite what some people think, The FBI is not without its resources. Our people have been working around the clock on these cases and it has now paid off rather handsomely I think." Mayfield allowed himself a smile of satisfaction, "Federal prosecutors feel the case is a very strong one. We have the murder weapon; it was behind the seat of her truck when we picked her up at work this morning," He looked briefly at the report, "A .243 caliber hunting rifle. Ballistics says the bullet taken from Hoffman's body was also a .243. It was a fast expanding hunting round, but enough of the base was left to get a match on the marks from the rifling. I'm betting it will prove to be from Martha Keyoni's gun."

Here the FBI agent opened another folder and consulted a paper, before concluding with a grim smile, "Her husband has given a sworn statement she was not at home at the time of the shooting, and that he doesn't know where she was. He admitted to Agent Smith that she had known for some time about Karl Hoffman's part in the desecration of ruins along the new highway route and, his part in supplying her son with drugs in return for artifacts."

Charlie Yazzie glanced sideways at Billy Red Clay, "You didn't know any of this, Billy?"

"Not until just this moment." Billy frowned at the FBI man, "It seems like you could have let me know this a tad earlier instead of letting me come in here looking like a dummy?"

Mayfield was unapologetic, "The reports went out earlier this morning, and they're probably on your desk as we speak... You too, Charlie, I personally made a point of seeing you got one." With a grim smile and wave of his hand the federal agent dismissed any further culpability and continued, "The prosecutor insisted it all be kept very hush, hush. We didn't want this out before we make our second arrest this morning."

Charlie's eyes widened. "A second arrest? Who might that be...and for what?"

"The murder of James Erdric."

"I thought you already had Jimmy John under arrest for Erdric's murder?" Charlie was stunned.

"We do have Mr. Jimmy John under arrest, but there was another person involved. The prosecutor is calling it a conspiracy."

Charlie lowered an eyelid at the agent, "I'm guessing you aren't going to tell us who the second person is you are going to arrest?"

"No, not just yet," Mayfield admitted and smiled while tapping the desk with a finger to emphasize his point. "But we will soon, I promise you that."

~~~~~~~

Billy Red Clay followed the Legal Services Investigator out to their units, parked in the shade of the Federal Building. "Well, that's just something, isn't it? They weren't kidding when they said they weren't going to put up with any more leaks from Tribal." Billy slapped his hat against his leg. "You'd a thought they'd tell me though…I'm the goddamned Liaison Office for Christ sake."

"Yes, well, at least we know where we stand now Billy, and no mistake." Charlie half-grinned at the policeman, "On the bright side, this should finally let you off the hook in the Hoffman thing."

Billy grinned too, "You're right, I was so mad I didn't even think of that." Billy Red Clay put his hat on, smiled and flicked the brim with a forefinger. "I'm going back to the office and tell Captain Beyale I want back on patrol duty." He hesitated and then shot Charlie quick glance, "I wonder if Beyale had any clue about the arrests before we did?"

"That, my friend is something we will probably never know." Charlie's mind was already chewing on the thought of the other arrest…the one Mayfield said was yet to come, and thought to himself, *I think my dropped ball is about to come back into play.*

"I hope the Captain didn't know. Beyale has always been a good boss, and a fair one too. I would hate to throw that away." Billy Red Clay was known for his penchant for giving credit where credit was due.

"Billy, how would you like to take a little run out to Martha Keyoni's place with me?" Charlie grinned, "I might need a little official back-up this morning."

"Martha Keyoni? She's locked up according to Mayfield." Billy wasn't sure what Charlie meant.

"It's not about Martha. I'd like to have a little talk with her husband, Hank, and her daughter Luanne, too. It surprises me Hank didn't stand up for Martha in this thing. There has to be more to it than what I heard in the FBI report."

Billy Red Clay didn't hesitate, "Sure, I've got a few hours to kill this morning; I don't have to be back in the office until this afternoon." The police-man nodded, "I'll ride along with you, but it's not going to be a happy place out there I'll bet you that."

"No, probably not, but I'll bet Agent Fred Smith is already on his way out there. They would be wise to send Fred Smith; he grew up in this country and knows the Navajo better than most."

~~~~~~

On the drive out to the Keyoni camp Charlie Yazzie couldn't help but think how much Billy Red Clay was like his old friend, Samuel Shorthair, Billy had worked for the former Liaison Officer a little less than a year before his death, but had taken on a good bit of his old boss's thought processes and general attitude. Charlie believed the young officer might someday go far. *If I don't get him killed like I did Sam Shorthair.* Charlie had never really come to terms with the fact that he had been the one that talked the Lieutenant into going along on another one of his hunches…just as he had today. Rationally, he knew his friend's death was not his fault, and he knew Billy didn't blame him for it, either, but the thought was always there just the same.

Billy Red Clay hadn't said much since they left Farmington, but now, looking out the window at the Colorado Plateau, wondered out loud, "Do you really think there's anything we can learn from these people the FBI hasn't already asked?"

"Well, that's what we are about to find out, Billy. There's generally some difference between what a Navajo will tell an FBI man, and what they might say to another Navajo, even a Navajo Lawman." Charlie didn't mention he occasionally had to send Thomas Begay or Harley Ponyboy to talk to a witness in a Legal Aid case. There was a difference.

They were almost to the Keyoni's turnoff when Billy Red Clay remembered that according to Thomas, the Keyoni cousins were living in the camp now. He wondered if Charlie had taken that into account. Thomas once told him the pair was about on a par with Danny Hat but not as smart. Harley Ponyboy, on the other hand maintained the two cousins were considerably worse. Billy suspected they were about to find out and hoped he was up to it.

The camp, when they pulled up to the main hogan, appeared deserted, and as Billy Red Clay eased up to the door, Charlie tooted the horn twice more before someone finally came to the door. When Hank Keyoni opened it a crack he was drunk, otherwise he might have been able to slam it in Billy Red Clay's face. Billy got his foot in the door and bulled his way on in. Charlie was right behind him and the first thing that hit him was the acrid stench of vomit. As their eyes adjusted to the darkened interior they saw one of the cousins passed out on a cot against the far wall and the other of the pair slumped over the table on the other side of the room. Luanne was nowhere in sight.

Charlie Yazzie eased past the Tribal policeman who was still keeping a wary eye on Hank Keyoni. Hank stood eyeing them from the middle of the room cussing under his breath. "Where's Luanne, Hank?" Charlie tried to keep his voice calm but thought there might still be a slight tremor to it.

Hank shook his head and tried to focus. "That's what the FBI wanted to know, too," the elder Keyoni said with a dour grin. "They were here earlier and told us they had arrested Martha when she got to work this morning; said they wanted to talk to Luanne...but they didn't say why. I told Martha she had better leave well enough alone. 'Danny's dead,' I told her. 'There's nothing you can do to change that, so just leave it alone,' I said." Hank dropped his head. "She's been knowing what Danny and Luanne were doing for months now...and they thought they were so smart, too. 'That's when you should have done something about those two kids,' I told her. 'Back when they were still young.' But there's no talking to her when she's in one of her moods." Hank got a sad little look on his face. "Now she's in jail and they didn't even say what for."

Billy Red Clay pushed right up in front of Hank and despite the man's bad breath, got right in his face. "She's in jail for murder Hank, and I doubt they're through with you people yet. What did they want to question Luanne about?"

"I a'ready told you I don't know," Hank replied, his voice steady but sullen. "They just needed to talk to her they said. I told them I didn't know where she was... She didn't come home last night."

Charlie moved in, "She didn't say where she was going? Yesterday, I mean when she left the house?"

"Naa, she didn't say, she never does, just comes and goes, never tells anyone anything. That's the kind of girl she is." Hank was still drunk, but not nearly as bad as he had been earlier. "I think there's something we need to get straight right now." He looked at both lawmen and lifted his chin, "Me and Martha are about through...have been for awhile now. She was moving back to her Hopi relatives—her son was going to go with her she said." Hank shook his head, "After Danny died she just sort of went crazy; said several times, someone was going to pay for him going the way he did. And she thinks Luanne is partially responsible too, she thought Luanne was the one who got Danny started." Hank's shoulders slumped, "She thinks Luanne might even be a witch." The man turned slightly away and Charlie thought he saw a tear slide down his cheek.

Billy Red Clay asked in a softer voice, "Hank is there anywhere you think Luanne could be? Who's she been going with lately?"

Hank thought a moment before turning back to them, his voice angry. "It's like I don't even know Luanne anymore; she has been acting like she's living in some other world. She says she don't have any boyfriends. Hank stopped right there, as though he thought he might already have said too much but then seemed unable to quit talking. "She's mentioned a few times that she needs to make up with an old friend, but hell, I don't even know who that would be."

Charlie looked at Billy Red Clay and nodded. The Tribal officer turned toward the door. "Hank, the FBI will likely be back at some point, you boys had best get this place cleaned up and the booze out of here before they come, or you'll all be in jail."

Charlie nodded briefly at Hank as he passed and then followed Billy out the door.

Back in the truck, Billy Red Clay let out a long slow breath. "I guess that explains a lot of things. Like you said earlier, I couldn't figure out why Hank didn't stand up for his wife. Now maybe I understand a little more where he's coming from."

Charlie nodded, "At this point it doesn't seem like Hank's involved in any of it—he seems to want that made plain right up front." He started the truck, but watched the hogan in his rear view mirror, wondering what would become of the Keyonis' now. "I guess the next question is where Luanne has taken herself off to. The FBI must know something or they wouldn't be coming out here to question her. Not to say she's being targeted in the murder, but I imagine there's some reason they made this their first stop this morning." Charlie didn't like it, but he said it anyway, "I wonder if Martha's been talking to them?"

Charlie's truck was still a good distance from the highway when the men spotted a government car parked at the turnoff.

Charlie turned to the policeman, "Looks like someone's watching the place."

Billy Red Clay snorted, "Or...they knew those people out here were through talking to them, followed us figuring we might do better."

Nosing the truck up to the government car, the two Navajo were surprised to see Agent Fred Smith get out and head back to Billy's side of the truck. The tribal policeman rolled down the window and put on a smile for the FBI man. Fred was all right in his book, he was just glad it wasn't Mayfield.

"How are you, Billy?" The agent looked across at Charlie Yazzie with a wave of his hand, "You doing all right Charlie?" Both men nodded in return and waited for Smith to continue. "I'm waiting for Mayfield, he's determined to see what he can get out of the Keyonis. I was halfway back to town when he called and said I should turn around...wait for him here. He didn't know you boys were out here of course, but I doubt that would have made a difference. Eldon's been talking to someone about the Keyoni girl...apparently has reason to believe she's connected to the Erdric murder." The agent saw the looks on their faces and was quick to add; "You boys have probably already heard what old man Keyoni's willing to tell and I doubt Mayfield will come up with anything better." Fred paused and looked from one to the other, "If there's any way you can help us out on this one it would be appreciated. Mayfield may not be here much longer and I think he wants to go out on a high note. This is important to him–could have a major bearing on his next posting." He smiled, "I don't think that's going to be New York."

Charlie leaned across Billy to look up at the agent. "We were sort of hoping you would be the next agent in charge out here."

Billy nodded, and added, "We're on this, Fred and if there's any way we can help make that happen you can count on us. Right now I doubt we know any more than you people do…maybe not as much actually, but like Mayfield, we are not without our resources."

The FBI man stroked his chin and nodded. "I'm not going to say anything about seeing you boys out here today." The agent turned to go but then paused. "It's time our agencies worked together for a change, it's not a contest."

Back on the highway, Billy Red Clay smiled as Charlie took a cutoff leading back to Farmington with less likelihood of running into Mayfield. He liked the idea of Fred Smith at the helm of the Bureau's local office, made a mental note not to be too hasty in giving up his place as Liaison Officer…not just yet anyway. A thought occurred to the young officer that made him uncomfortable. "Who do you suppose was the little bird that made Mayfield aware of this information regarding Luanne Keyoni?"

"I can't even imagine, unless Martha thinks her daughter will testify against her in the murder of Karl Hoffman."

Charlie left Billy Red Clay off at his truck in Farmington, then on a whim decided to drop by Professor Custer's small office facility. Someone, he thought, should be finishing up the sorting and packing of specimens from the dig. When he opened the door he was surprised to see the entire crew there, Thomas and Harley were crating things up and old man Paul T'Sosi was putting labels on the boxes. George Custer was at his desk speaking to someone on the phone and didn't look up as the investigator entered.

Only Harley Ponyboy glanced at him and smiled, then gave a little salute before saying, "Well, looky who's here, just in time ta help load the trailer, too."

Thomas raised his head at this and asked, "What have you been up to today? Not wasting the taxpayers money on wild goose chases, I hope?"

Charlie grinned. "I guess that's debatable, it doesn't feel like I accomplished much, but that remains to be seen, I suppose." Charlie looked around the room and appeared to think about his next question, "Anyone seen anything of Luanne Keyoni the last day or so?" No one answered; that was the Navajo way of saying they didn't know anything.

Paul T'Sosi looked across at the investigator and changed the subject. "You and Billy Red Clay catch any crooks today?" The old man smiled at the surprised look on Charlie's face, "I saw you two leaving town as I came in with my daughter this morning. We waved but you must not have seen us."

"No, I guess we didn't. We were on our way out to the Keyoni place." Charlie watched Harley's face as he said this, and thought he saw a slight tightening of the man's jaw, and just for a second felt sure he was going to say something. If that was Harley's intention he apparently thought better of it. He didn't look Charlie's way and continued wrapping bits of pottery.

Paul moved around the table and was quite close to Charlie when he whispered, "I think Lucy was on her way out to see Sue when she dropped me off... What are those two up to? They're on the phone all day long." He paused and canted his head to one side.

214

"She tells me you and Sue are having trouble?" The old man didn't seem embarrassed to bring this up.

Charlie rolled his eyes and looked annoyed at the old singer. He knew the old man wouldn't have asked if it weren't already common knowledge.

"Like everyone else I guess, Paul, we have a few little problems but nothing serious…nothing to be concerned about." Charlie knew the old man saw through him and was instantly sorry he'd said anything at all.

Paul T'Sosi smiled and considered the younger man with a calculating eye. "I'm just asking because I'm the one who married you—at least the Navajo part of it. I would hate to think I did a bad job of sticking you two together."

"No, you didn't do a bad job; it'll be fine. I'm working on it." Charlie owed the old man this much, and knew he had only inquired out of an honest concern. The investigator tended to listen more closely to what Paul had to say these days, and again resolved to broach the subject with Sue when he got home that night. They would get whatever the problem was out in the light and fix it. "By the way Paul, when was the last time Luanne Keyoni came out to your place?"

Paul didn't hesitate. "Oh, I guess it was about three or four days ago. She still wants to do that cleansing. Funny thing though, she ask me if it could cure someone of being a witch, she's a strange one. I'm glad Harley didn't get hooked up with her."

George Custer finished his phone call and finally looked up to acknowledge Charlie Yazzie. "That was Eldon Mayfield on the phone. He said I might be interested to hear that they have a warrant out for

William Crawley and wondered if I knew where they might find him. He's going to be charged with trafficking in illegal antiquities, he said." The professor chuckled, "Not that it surprises me; it's been a long time coming. He also asked if I would be willing to testify concerning what I knew of Crawley's business. I told him I didn't know how much help I would be but let him know I was happy to oblige."

Charlie now understood Mayfield's good humor that morning. It appeared things were going his way. Eldon Mayfield was on a roll, and this caused Charlie to wonder how the head agent made out at the Keyoni camp with Hank and his two nephews. He was fairly certain those boys had been no help.

After Charlie said his goodbyes, Harley Ponyboy followed him out to his truck, then just stood there, obviously uncertain how to go about what he had to say. Charlie turned to him and almost smiled at the look on the little man's face. "What is it Harley? ...Just spit it out, I need to get home."

"Uh...well, maybe you could give me a ride home... I know it's out of the way but I need ta talk to you about something...you know, a little legal advice. Thomas has ta take the old man ta see a sick person and that might take half the night. I don't have no way home."

Charlie Yazzie could see there was more to it than this and his curiosity was aroused. "Okay, Harley, jump in the truck; I don't have all night, it's been a long day and I have stuff to take care of at home."

About halfway to his place Harley started talking and soon had Charlie Yazzie's full attention.

"Luanne's out at my place Charlie, and she's scared." Harley's eyes grew wider as he went on, "She says her brother introduced her ta James Erdric and he knew right away she was a druggie, just like Danny. It was her and Erdric and William Crawley that was up at the ruins the night the amulet was stolen. Erdric wanted her involved so he would have something on her that would keep her quiet should it come ta law problems."

Charlie was having a hard time taking all this in and eyed Harley suspiciously. "And you believe all this Harley?" It almost sounded like the story was being made up as his friend went along.

"Oh, I believe it all right Charlie. Luanne said she didn't have no place else ta go, that's why she came to me. You'll see when you hear for yourself."

"Does she know you're telling me all this?"

Harley wrung his hands as he went on, "No, she don't know, I didn't know I was going to tell you myself until you showed up at the Doc's place this afternoon. What else was I supposed to do? I'm telling you she's afraid." Harley looked tired and leaned against the side window. "There may be more to this story than she's saying Charlie. Luanne says she has no way out now. I'm afraid what she might do to herself."

Charlie's mind was racing. The pieces were beginning to fall into place; Luanne had been the key after all. "So what happened with Erdric getting shot? How'd that happen?"

Harley thought a moment before getting back on track, "I was coming ta that. Crawley stayed in his car while Luanne and Erdric went up to the *kiva*. She says Erdric had been spying on us the whole time, and was sure we'd made a serious find." Harley licked his lips, rubbed his nose, and became even more agitated, "Crawley wanted ta be there. He had long suspected Erdric had another buyer on the hook and probably had already sold him several choice pieces. According to Luanne, he was determined not ta lose out this time."

"So, Crawley was the head of the organization from the start?"

"I guess so. None of it makes any sense to me, Luanne says she and Erdric must have dropped a little bowl they wrapped up and put in a jacket pocket. Erdric was very upset about that. He planned to put Crawley off by offering him the bowl then keep the amulet for himself. He hid a pocket full of beads along with the amulet." Harley fell silent now to catch his breath and consider the rest of the story.

Thinking about it Charlie figured Crawley guessed there was more than the two looters reported, and probably thought they were lying when they said they had lost a nice bowl coming down from the *kiva*. That there was nothing to show for the risky midnight excursion must have infuriated the man.

Harley turned to him as though reading his thoughts. "Luanne said Crawley was pissed and threatened James Erdric ta the point the man became scared and just stopped talking. Luanne said they were not far from the road construction camp when Crawley pulled his suburban over ta the side of the road and went around to Erdric's side...pulled him out of the truck. Erdric broke away and hit the ground running. That's when Crawley pulled out a small pistol and fired several shots after him; Luanne stayed in the truck, scared she would be next. But Crawley only took her out ta the main highway and dropped her off not far from home. He warned her to keep her mouth shut no matter what happened. If she didn't, he said, he'd kill her. She knew he'd do it too.

"So, it was Crawley that shot Erdric but apparently only wounded him? Jimmy John later finished him off with a knife...in his own trailer?"

"Luanne thinks that's how it must have happened, I guess." Harley saw his turnoff coming up and pointed with his chin, though Charlie was already slowing the truck.

It was getting on toward dark when they pulled into the yard and noticed there was no light in the trailer. Harley's broken down truck sat forlornly to one side; he was a poor mechanic and Thomas had not yet been persuaded to have a look at it. The little man gave Charlie a quick glance and frowned. "I'm pretty sure Luanne don't go ta bed this early...you'd think she'd at least leave a light on."

"Maybe she doesn't want to attract attention."

"Maybe... She did park her truck down in the wash so nobody could see it from the road." Harley didn't like the look of it and opened the glove box where Charlie kept his revolver; taking it out he passed it over to the investigator without saying a word. Charlie decided it might not be a bad idea under the circumstances, though he had no idea what those circumstances might turn out to be.

Harley eased the truck door open and stood for a moment surveying the familiar scene for the slightest thing out of place. Something was wrong; he was sure of it. Charlie was out of the truck and moving toward the trailer and Harley was right beside him to open the door—at that exact instant, they heard the sound of an engine start up beyond the trailer. Harley exclaimed, "Luanne's truck is parked in the wash!" Both men started running toward the sound thinking Luanne had spotted Charlie's truck pulling in and was making a break for it. As they rounded the front of the trailer they could see a dark-colored SUV roaring down the dry watercourse, spewing sand and fishtailing from side to side. They could make out the form of a driver at the wheel but saw no one else inside.

Harley shook his head, "That's not Luanne's truck. Her truck's still down there."

Charlie whirled and headed back to the trailer with Harley close behind.

"Harley, you go check on Luanne; see if she's all right. I'm going to try and cut that car off before it hits the highway!" Charlie shouted over his shoulder as he ran. Harley Ponyboy changed direction in midstride, cutting back toward the trailer. Charlie Yazzie whipped his truck around and headed for the big road. As he came onto the highway he could make out the vehicle coming down the wash, apparently slowed by the deep sand and failing light. He smiled to himself, *He's not from around here or he would know to stay to the high side of the wash.* Charlie had no more than thought this when the SUV ground to a halt, temporarily mired to the front hubs. The driver put it in reverse and was able to pull free and angle over to harder ground, but too late. He could see Charlie's truck swerve into the wash from the highway. That way was now blocked! By the time he had inched the car around and headed back the way he had come the tribal unit was on him, lights flashing, and siren at full blast. The driver thought he might still get around Luanne's truck, and back up to the road, but when his vehicle again bogged down he knew it was over and threw open his door. Pulling out a pistol, he knelt behind the door to fire at the Tribal unit.

Charlie swerved as the first bullet shattered the windshield; he considered it a miracle he wasn't hit. The shooter's second round glanced off the bumper, but by that time Charlie had the truck sideways and rolled out the off side. He fired his own revolver from beneath his unit but saw no evidence of a hit. He did see Harley Ponyboy coming on a dead run from the trailer waving his old single barrel shotgun. When Harley reached the bank above the SUV he let go with a load of Number 8 shot which he kept for rabbits. Thomas had told him the shot was too small for rabbits, but Harley liked to cover a lot of ground.

The shot peppered the SUV from front to back; the shooter behind the door yelped and turned to fire back at Harley. Charlie fired first and plunked the 160 grain round right into the middle of the door. The car's window was rolled up so that protection was lost, allowing the bullet to smash through and into his assailant's shoulder, causing him to drop his weapon. Harley was on him fast, and gave him a good whack with the butt of his shotgun. Charlie, too, was there in an instant and the two Navajo dragged the man to his feet. He was a stranger to both of them and not the sort you would expect to put up so determined a fight.

The man was was older, nearly bald, and wore thick glasses.

Charlie's first words were directed to Harley, "How's Luanne? She all right?"

Harley shot a deadly glance at their prisoner and backhanded him across the face. "She will be when she gets over the beating this sorry sonofabitch gave her." When he drew back to hit the man again, Charlie reached over and caught his arm.

"He's had enough for now; leave him here with me and go on back to the trailer...see what you can do for Luanne." He had seldom seen his friend so riled and thought it best he keep the man out of Harleys reach. Their prisoner appeared not to be hurt too badly but it was plain the fight had gone out of him. The bullet only clipped his shoulder and it was barely bleeding.

When tribal ran the plates on the SUV Charlie was not surprised to find he had arrested the notorious William Crawley, a taciturn man who had not spoken a word since he was shot. The dispatcher said Billy Red Clay was on his way and advised that the FBI were already notified. Back in the trailer, Charlie cuffed Crawley's hands behind his back in a kitchen chair, then helped Harley do what they could to make Luanne comfortable. She had recovered somewhat and sat glowering from blackened eyes—her nose was oddly bent. Harley couldn't stop looking at it. "The rescue unit is on its way, Luanne. They'll fix you up in no time...and I wouldn't worry about that nose. I've had mine broke two or three times, and look at me."

Luanne turned her face to Harley and glared, "Just shut up Harley—I don't want to look like you." Then her voice softened and she attempted a crooked smile. "Thanks for getting here when you did. That bastard said he was going to beat me to death. I thought for a while he already had."

Harley smiled shyly, "Aww, that's all right, Luanne—I doubt he was man enough ta beat *you* to death anyway."

~~~~~~

It was late that night when Billy Red Clay dropped Charlie off at his little house in Waterflow. He'd had Dispatch call the house before leaving Harley's and Sue was waiting up. Dispatch hadn't told her much and she was relieved to see her husband unharmed and in good spirits, seemingly elated over the outcome of the night's adventures.

"This will be a feather in the cap of Tribal authorities." Charlie told Sue, holding her tight. "I think we've got this one wrapped up and if we can convince Luanne to turn State's evidence in the Erdric killing—she might get off pretty light. I'll make sure she knows that. Otherwise, she'll be charged as a co-conspirator and face some very serious charges." He smiled, "I think it's a no-brainer. The only one she'll hurt at his point is William Crawley and I'm sure she'll be up for that. The FBI already has enough evidence on Jimmy John to send him up for a very long time." And as far as Karl Hoffman's murder goes, the FBI thinks they have Martha Keyoni dead to rights. She'll likely spend a good many years away, though there are mitigating circumstances that could lighten her sentence somewhat."

Sue finally backed away with a searching look at her husband then moved toward the stove. "I have your dinner in the oven...maybe then you can fill me in on the details. After that, you and I have a few other things to talk about." This would have sounded more ominous, had Charlie not been caught up in the moment. This was a mistake he would soon come to regret.

Sue brought his dinner along with a cup of coffee for each of them and than sat across the table watching him eat through hooded eyes; there was but little else to betray her thoughts.

Charlie finished his meal and launched into a full account of what happened at Harley Ponyboy's camp. Sue listened, nodding from time to time, raising her eyebrows at the part where gunfire broke out, then frowned and shook her head. As Charlie continued he realized Sue had not said a word, nor had she questioned any part of the story, which was unlike her. His telling of the tale gradually tapered off with a few comments on what effect all this might have on those involved. The pair then sat in silence, regarding one another almost warily as they waited for what was to come.

"I'm pregnant!" Sue said this so forcefully her husband was taken aback and for a moment said nothing, surprised, but hoping this was the full extent of the problem.

The thought Sue might be pregnant had crossed his mind several times over the last few weeks, but he had brushed it aside as unlikely, thinking *surely she surely would have said something.* Sue had always been strong natured and the first one to speak her mind should the occasion call for it. Now it was out in the open. Charlie felt there must be good reason for keeping the secret this long and opened his mouth to ask…

Sue burst into tears unable to hold back any longer and at the same time unleashed a tirade on her husband. "You have been so wrapped up in these murders you haven't said a dozen words to me in days." Sue sniffled though she wasn't the sort to seek pity. "When Joseph Wiley was born and we had such a hard time of it, you said we probably shouldn't have another child. It could be dangerous, you said. And later, even after that curse was taken off, you still said it wasn't a good idea. I knew this was something you wouldn't want to hear."

Charlie interrupted, "It had nothing to do with the so-called *curse*. I just didn't want you to go through that trauma again. The doctor said at the time we nearly lost Joseph Wiley, and that you were in danger too… He admitted it could happen again… Might even be a genetic thing as far as he knew." Charlie was regaining his composure and beginning to suspect this whole thing was not quite so much his fault… at least not as much as he first thought. Still he was aware he owned some responsibility in the matter. Sue's more traditional mindset had entered into it as well, and in his opinion that was partially responsible. When he went so far as to say this to her, it didn't help…it didn't help at all. Sue stood and made as if to leave the room.

Charlie rose, too, took her arm and admitted, "Sue, that doctor was young and inexperienced— maybe didn't know what he was talking about. I've thought about it a lot over the last several years and realize now he was probably mistaken." He gathered himself and took a deep breath. "Sue a baby is fine with me! I think Joseph Wiley needs a brother... Or sister." He drew her close and whispered in her ear, "If this is what you want, then it's what I want too."

After a few moments, Sue moved back and stared long and hard at her husband. With a wise and gentle look, she searched his face before speaking, "Then this is the way it will be and we will start again from here."

Charlie nodded and let out a long sigh. "Good," he smiled, "Paul T'Sosi was afraid he had not stuck us together as well as he should."

Sue also smiled, imagining the old singer sticking them together with prayers and pollen. "Well I did think he was a little stingy with the blue corn- meal." Both of them chuckled.

Sue brightened as she left to check on their son, and then threw back over her shoulder, "I can't wait to tell Lucy what's happened in those murder cases," ...leaving Charlie Yazzie standing in the middle of the room...with one finger held up in silent protest.

~~~~~~

It was almost a week before things quieted down, and though the Professor spent most of that time out at the dig, it finally came time to gather at the *kiva* and finish the job of closing down the site. Charlie,

Thomas and Harley stood ready to back-fill the chamber with rubble and large stones from the alcove. But before they did, the professor knelt to remove the stone slab hiding the burial, then set aside the shallow inverted bowl from the shrouded figure…the girl they called the Swallow Keeper. Reaching in his pocket, George brought out the turquoise amulet and studied it a final moment before placing it back exactly as it had been found. He then replaced the bowl, and all was as it had been for a thousand years.

"It's not all about the science," the professor whispered turning to the others. "This was a real person, living a life we scarce can understand. She had almost nothing. It's not right to take away what little she had." He stood and smiled at a solemn Harley Ponyboy, who stood silently contemplating the grave he had found. "We know what we need to know about her—within the current limits of our ability. One day, when the science has progressed, someone will have another look…see things we cannot now imagine. Then perhaps more of her story will come to light, but for now we know enough. We will let her go back to sleep."

The End

Wolves of Winter

ABOUT THE AUTHOR

Writer/Poet R. Allen Chappell's work has appeared in magazines, literary and poetry publications, and has been featured on public radio and television. He grew up in New Mexico at the edge of the great reservation.

Books in the Navajo Nation Mystery Series listed in order include:

Navajo Autumn
Boy Made of Dawn
Ancient Blood
Mojado
Magpie Speaks
Wolves of Winter

Be sure to check out the new audio book series of selected Navajo Nation Mysteries, now available on our Amazon book pages, and in Public Libraries, as well as on Audible and in many retail outlets.

The author and his wife call western Colorado home where he continues to pursue a lifelong interest in the prehistory of the Four Corners region. Reader's comments are welcome at: rachappell@yahoo.com

If you've enjoyed this book, please consider going to its Amazon book page to leave a short review. It would be most appreciated.

Glossary

1. *Aa'a'ii* — Magpie
2. *Acheii* — Grandfather *
3. *Ashkii Ana'dlohi* — Laughing boy
4. *A-hah-la'nih* — affectionate greeting*
5. *Billigaana* — white people
6. *Ch'ihónit't* — *a spirit path flaw*
7. *Chindi* — (or chinde) Spirit of the dead *
8. *Diné* — Navajo people
9. *Diné Bikeyah* — Navajo country
10. *Hataalii* — Shaman (Singer)*
11. *Hastiin* — (Hosteen) Man or Mr. *
12. *hogan* — (Hoogahn) dwelling or house
13. *Hozo* — To walk in beauty *
14. *Ma'iitsoh* — *Wolf*
15. *Shimásáni* — grandmother
16. *Shiyé* — *Cousin/brother*
17. Shizhé'é — Father *
18. *Tsé Bii' Ndzisgaii* — Monument Valley
19. *Yaa' eh t'eeh* — Greeting; Hello
20. *Yeenaaldiooshii* — Skinwalker; witch*

*See Notes

Wolves of Winter

R. Allen Chappell

Notes

1. *Acheii* — Grandfather – there are several words for Grandfather, depending on how formal the intent and the gender of the speaker.

2. *Aa'a'ii* — Long known as a trickster or "thief of little things." It is thought Magpie can speak and sometimes brings messages from the beyond.

4. *A-hah-la'nih* — A greeting: affectionate version of Yaa' eh t'eeh, generally only used among family and close friends.

7. *Chindi* — When a person dies inside a hogan, it is said that his chindi or spirit remains there forever, causing the hogan to be abandoned. Chindi are not considered benevolent entities. For the traditional Navajo, just speaking a dead person's name may call up his chindi and cause harm to the speaker or others.

10. *Hataalii* — Generally known as a "Singer" among the Diné, these men are considered "Holy Men" and have apprenticed to older practitioners— sometimes for many years—to learn the ceremonies. They make the sand paintings that are an integral part of the healing and know the many songs that must be sung in the correct order.

11. *Hastiin* — The literal translation is "man" but is often considered the word for "Mr." as well. "Hosteen" is the usual version Anglos use.

13. *Hozo* — For the Navajo "hozo" (sometimes hozoji) is a general state of well-being, both physical and spiritual, that indicates a certain "state of grace," which is referred to as "walking in beauty." Illness or depression is the usual cause of "loss of hozo," which may put one out of sync with the people as a whole. There are ceremonies to restore hozo and return the ailing person to a oneness with the people.

14. *Ma'iitsoh* — The Navajo Wolf is yet another reference to one of the many forms a witch can take, something like a werewolf in this instance.

17. *Shizhé'é* — (or *Shih-chai*) There are several words for "Father," depending on the degree of formality intended and sometimes even the gender of the speaker.

20. *Yeenaaldiooshii* — These witches, as they are often referred to, are the chief source of evil or fear in traditional Navajo superstitions. They are thought to be capable of many unnatural acts, such as flying or turning themselves into werewolves and other ethereal creatures; hence the term Skinwalkers, referring to their ability to change forms or skins.

40926141R00138

Made in the USA
Middletown, DE
27 February 2017